Strange Powers
of the Human Mind

Herbie Brennan

Illustrated by The Maltings Partnership

faber and faber

First published in 2006 by Faber and Faber Limited
3 Queen Square, London WC1N 3AU

Designed by Planet Creative, Andy Summers
Editorial Management: Paula Borton
Illustrated by The Maltings Partnership

Printed in England by Bookmarque Ltd

Herbie Brennan is hereby identified as author of this work in
accordance with Section 77 of the Copyright, Designs and
Patents Act 1988

A CIP record for this book is available from the British
Library

ISBN 0571 223168

2 4 6 8 10 9 7 5 3 1

Contents

Chapter 1   The wolf that Stalin couldn't tame   9

Chapter 2   The wizard of Vienna   20

Chapter 3   You are feeling sleepy...   29

Chapter 4   Hypnotic powers   36

Chapter 5   Super memory   43

Chapter 6   Weird talents   51

Chapter 7   Artificial reincarnation   60

Chapter 8   The Willing Game   73

Chapter 9   Mind control   88

Chapter 10   Beyond hypnosis   100

Chapter 11   Magic of the mind   113

Chapter 12   Creatures of the mind   117

Chapter 13   'Skyring in the spirit vision'   127

Chapter 14   Giving up the ghost   137

Chapter 15   Fear of floating   147

Chapter 16   Table-turning   157

Chapter 17   The power of mind   172

Chapter 18   Full circle   184

You can do it   190

For Jacks, whose own strange powers are mentioned later in this book.

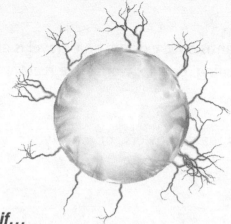

What if...

... you can't trust your teachers? What if you can't believe your parents?

What if...

... the things you know for sure are just plain wrong?

What if...

... scientists sometimes just *make up* the answers?

What if...

... the world is not the way you think it is? What if physics is all lies? What if the stuff they tell you is impossible keeps happening every day?

What if…

… Atlantis once existed, time travel is already happening, parallel worlds are real?

What if…

… *you* have powers beyond your wildest dreams?

Chapter 1

The wolf that Stalin couldn't tame

The year was 1937. The Nazi Party was in power in Germany. The storm clouds of war were gathering over Europe as Hitler's demands became more and more outrageous. And in neutral Poland, an entertainer known for his weird mental abilities made a startling prediction. Facing a 1,000-strong audience from the stage of a Warsaw theatre, the mentalist Wolf Messing uttered nine words that would come close to costing him his life, *'Hitler will die if he turns toward the East!'*

It's not recorded what the audience made of this prophecy, but Hitler himself took it very seriously. When word reached the Führer in Germany, he promptly placed a 200,000 reichmark bounty on

Messing's head – a fortune in the money values of the day. Messing wasn't too worried. There was little love lost between Berlin and Warsaw, no cooperation at all between the two, so he felt himself safe in his native land. But then, on September 1, 1939, Reich armies invaded Poland and, using the new military technique of *blitzkrieg*, overran the country in days. Messing knew he was in big trouble and went into hiding in a Warsaw meat locker. But he couldn't stay in hiding forever and one night when he ventured onto the streets of the capital, he was stopped by a Nazi officer.

The Nazi consulted his pocketbook of wanted photographs, then asked Messing who he was. Messing tried to pretend he was an artist, but the Nazi knew his identity perfectly well: "You're the man who predicted the death of the Führer!" Then he grabbed Messing by the hair and struck him in the mouth, smashing six of his teeth.

Messing was dragged off to the nearest police station where it soon became clear he was facing a death penalty. For most men it would have been only a matter of time, but Messing had a secret weapon. Over his years as a mentalist, he had worked to develop some strange powers of his mind. Now, with his very life at stake, he decided to put them to the test.

In a scene worthy of a fantasy movie, he began to concentrate. For a moment, nothing happened. Then, slowly, every policeman in the station, including the Nazi officer who had taken him in and the sentry guarding the exit, began to move like zombies into the room where Messing was being held.

Partly to aid his concentration, partly to ensure there were no distractions, Messing lay down on the floor and grew still as death. But as soon as the room was filled, he leaped to his feet, raced out and locked the door. Then he fled for the Russian border.

He crossed into Brest Litovsk (a major city in Belarus, then part of the Soviet Union, now known simply as Brest), a town swollen by refugees fleeing from the Polish occupation. There he paused to take stock. He was penniless and alone (his entire family was later slaughtered by the Nazis in the Warsaw Ghetto). Worse still, he could not even speak the language. He decided his first priority was to find a job. To that end, he presented himself at the Ministry of Culture.

Messing's qualifications were, to say the least, unusual. He had spent his life working as a psychic, giving 'readings' to personal clients and demonstrating mystic powers – mainly telepathy – on stage. Ministry officials were not impressed. They told him firmly there was no room for fortune-tellers or sorcerers in Soviet Russia ... and that telepathy didn't exist! As he'd done weeks earlier in the Polish police station, Messing began to concentrate... The result was a job with the Ministry of Culture itself, incredibly touring Belarus to give demonstrations in the art of telepathy.

The form his demonstrations took was dramatic. Typically, the audience was asked to elect a special jury, then decide on something they wanted Messing to do. Messing was then required to find out psychically what was wanted. The sealed instructions were delivered to the jury, who had the job of judging whether Messing performed his task correctly.

On one occasion his task was to find a particular doctor in the audience and, using scissors, cut out a picture of a dog from a sponge in the doctor's pocket. Messing walked down the aisle, found the doctor, took scissors and sponge from his pocket, then announced that since he didn't want to cut up the man's sponge, he proposed to draw an outline of a dog on it using chalk.

Although Messing managed feats of this type time and time again, the official Soviet stance was that he used trickery or at very least a difficult technique known as 'muscle-reading' where involuntary movements of a subject's muscles would lead Messing to his target.

MUSCLE READING

Muscle reading is a psychological trick that can, if performed properly, give the impression you have astonishing telepathic powers. Typically, this is the way the trick is performed:

Have your friends hide a small object

somewhere in a room while you are absent. Tell them you will use your mystic abilities to find it and challenge them to use the strength of their collective mind to try to prevent your doing so.

After you enter the room, have them blindfold you securely and test the blindfold to ensure you can see nothing at all. With one of their number linking your arm so you don't trip, you begin to criss-cross the room until, eventually, you announce you've found the hidden object.

It looks like magic, but in fact all you are doing is paying attention to the subtle muscle movements of the person holding your arm. Since the whole group has been challenged to stop you, he or she will unconsciously try to push you away from the hidden object when you get close.

> The movement is very subtle and difficult to detect, but once you get the hang of the technique you can virtually walk directly to the hidden object, to the absolute amazement of your friends.

But whatever the official line, Messing eventually had his strange powers confirmed by the most powerful – and hideously dangerous – Communist Party official in the country: Party Secretary-General and Head of State, Josef Stalin.

Stalin – the name means 'Man of Steel' – had risen to supreme power in Soviet Russia by murdering all his closest rivals. It was the start of a career marked by bloodshed of almost unimaginable proportions. He was the direct cause of even more deaths than Adolf Hitler, most of them his own people. Famously he was quoted as saying, "One death is a tragedy. A million deaths is a statistic." He was so feared by his colleagues that following his death in 1953, his body was left for days as terrified Party officials waited in case he might somehow revive.

Messing's first encounter with Stalin occurred in 1940. With the Soviet Union not yet involved in the Second World War, Moscow theatres remained open and Messing was performing in one of them when KGB (the Soviet Secret Service) officials mounted the stage, announced the show was over and dragged him away to a waiting car. He was taken to an unknown destination where Stalin questioned him about what had happened in Poland and what Messing thought Polish leaders might do in response to the Nazi invasion.

But it seemed that Stalin's interest in Wolf Messing wasn't entirely political. He'd heard of the man's remarkable powers and decided to put them to the test. He challenged Messing to use his psychic abilities to rob the Moscow Gosbank of 100,000 roubles. To rule out trickery Stalin made sure Messing was not known by anybody at the bank – and also insisted two state officials accompany him to witness the exact details of the robbery.

What Stalin's men reported back was astonishing. Messing walked into the bank armed only with a blank piece of paper torn from a school notebook and a small attaché case. He marched up to the nearest cashier, handed him the paper and opened the case. Nothing was said, but after a moment the cashier began to fill it with money. Messing brought the case over to his official minders, who counted the money and confirmed it was exactly 100,000 roubles. Satisfied Messing had carried out Stalin's instructions to the letter, they told him to return the cash. When Messing did so, the cashier looked at the case, then the blank note and promptly collapsed on the floor.

Spectacularly successful though it was, the test did not satisfy Stalin. He decided to try something else and had Messing brought to an inner room at the Kremlin then ordered three separate sets of security guards to ensure he did not leave the building. Minutes later, Messing was standing in the street outside waving up at the officials he'd easily left behind.

Perhaps one of the most remarkable aspects of this experiment was that Messing was allowed to live after it. Stalin was obsessed by security and

Messing had just proved he could walk past guard after guard without an exit pass. What was to stop him walking the other way ... and perhaps assassinating Stalin himself?

The answer, it seemed, was nothing. In an even more bizarre experiment, Messing set himself to enter, without official pass or any authorisation, Stalin's private dacha (country house) at Kuntsevo. Nowhere in the Soviet Union was more heavily guarded than the leader's residence. Every member of the staff was an official of the secret police. Armed patrols roamed the grounds outside.

But Messing walked calmly past them all. Incredibly, as he entered the building, security staff stood back and saluted him respectfully. He moved swiftly through several rooms before walking in on Stalin himself, who was dealing with State papers on a dining room table. How could all this happen?

The fact that Messing was a showman strongly suggests trickery of some kind or other. Stage demonstrations of strange mental powers are often – indeed usually – not what they seem, however impressive they may appear. But the point about a stage show is that the entertainer has control of his environment. He can set up the situation to suit himself, use secret props or stooges (people planted in the audience) and make whatever preparations he needs in advance of the show.

It's difficult to see how anything of this sort could have happened at Stalin's dacha where security was tighter than a drum. So even if Messing may have used trickery on stage, it may well be that he really did have an unusual ability of some description. Several observers are convinced they know what it was. They believe Wolf Messing used hypnosis.

Chapter 2

The wizard of Vienna

Although he never hypnotised anybody in his life, Franz Anton Mesmer is widely known as the 'Father of Hypnosis'. His story makes a stimulating study for anybody interested in strange powers.

He was born in Germany in 1734 in a district that now forms part of Switzerland. His parents were wealthy and young Mesmer proved clever, with the result that he eventually found a place in the University of Vienna. He got his degree at the age of 32 on the basis of his thesis – The Influence of the Planets on the Human Body.

Those were the days when astrology was still taught in the universities of Europe and it was commonly believed that planetary influences could play a part in medicine. But Mesmer had his own thoughts. His thesis shows he believed in the existence of a universal energy ocean that was subject to tides caused by the movements of the various planets.

So far he wasn't a million miles away from the standard thinking of the time, but Mesmer went a stage further and put forward the idea that these tides were what kept humans healthy. Furthermore, if there was a blockage of the tidal energy flow, sickness resulted.

It was enough to earn him his degree, but then a professor who was interested in his ideas discovered it was possible to cure stomach cramps by the application of a magnet[1]. He discussed the phenomenon with Mesmer and suggested that the magnet might be influencing the subtle energy Mesmer believed to circulate throughout the human body.

Mesmer by now was starting out on his chosen career as a doctor. Following common medical practice, he tried to cure his patients by the application of leeches and the use of the 'perpetual pill,' a pellet of metallic antimony used to treat constipation.

[1]For most of my life the idea that magnets could cure illness was dismissed as rubbish by the medical profession. In recent years, however, there have been signs of a change of mind. Experiments have shown that magnetic fields can speed up your rate of healing and so many people have discovered the effectiveness of magnetism for pain relief.

Both techniques worked rather better than you might think. Leeches excrete a substance that prevents blood clotting and is now being increasingly used to help stroke victims and heart patients, while it has been shown that (limited) blood loss stimulates the immune system. Metallic antimony moves through the digestive tract and irritates the bowel enough to cure constipation. In Mesmer's day, the chamber pot was typically searched for the pellet, which was then wiped off and put aside for future use. Perpetual pills of this type often passed through several generations of a family.

But despite his successes with standard practices, Mesmer took on the professor's idea and started to experiment with magnets. Lo and behold, magnetism did indeed reduce pain and, in Mesmer's opinion, influenced body processes in other ways. Then one day in 1775 came a breakthrough. While treating a patient with an open wound, he noticed that the blood flow increased every time he came close to the man, but slowed down again when he moved away. He started to think about it and came to the conclusion that his own body was acting like a magnet on the blood of the patient.

Before long he had gone so far as to publish his ideas in a pamphlet. In it he used the term that was to become famously associated with his name – animal magnetism. The medical profession didn't take to his ideas and when he began to use them to produce cures other doctors couldn't match, they responded by denouncing him as a quack. When patients continued to consult him (and leave his practice feeling considerably better) the medical profession responded by publishing savage – and often savagely unfair – satires.

Anton Mesmer

Mesmer pressed on regardless and eventually found himself with a member of the local aristocracy as a patient. The man suffered from chronic spasms and when Mesmer cured him, his fame spread dramatically. As his experience grew, Mesmer came to the conclusion that the magnetism you get from magnets and his own newly discovered 'animal magnetism' were one and the same thing – in other words, the human body generated a magnetic field. He turned his mind to inventing a mechanical apparatus that would increase and conduct the energy.

What he came up with was spectacular. He created an enormous wooden tub which he half filled with iron filings, then topped up with water. Into the mixture he sank a series of open jars packed with magnets. Then he set a long L-shaped metal rod into each jar so that it protruded through the side of his tub. What he ended up with – or so he believed – was a massive device that would hugely amplify the magnetism in the jars and conduct it into his patients.

A magnetism treatment from Mesmer at this time was fairly creepy. You were led into a darkened room where a hidden orchestra played low, spooky music. As your eyes gradually became accustomed to the gloom, you could just make out the shape of the huge tub … and the dim forms of your fellow patients clinging to the metal rods.

You took your place at your own rod, gripped it firmly and waited. The music gradually grew louder, more dramatic. Then, when expectation was at a fever pitch, Mesmer himself would appear, dressed in spectacular robes and carrying what he called a 'magnetic wand'. The Wizard of Vienna would then pass through the darkened room, touching one patient after another with his wand, or sometimes simply with his hands. Some sighed, some groaned, some screamed, but most fell down in a fit. And those were the ones who tended to get up again completely cured.

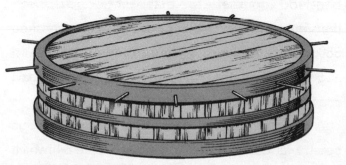

Mesmer's tub

The positive results did not help Mesmer's reputation with his fellow physicians and the criticism continued to grow. Word started to go round that this unorthodox doctor was using the whole business of 'magnetic passes' as an excuse to 'feel up' his female patients. Before long, he had a call from Austria's dreaded Morality Police.

Maybe Mesmer didn't trust the police, maybe he really had been misbehaving. In any case he declined to stick around for the investigation and fled Vienna for Paris where he quickly set up a practice that was to prove even more successful than the one he left behind. And not only successful, but fashionable – so much so that King Louis XVI offered him a pension. He began to teach his methods to others and soon had a great number of professional followers. Several of them banded together to establish a 'magnetic company.' It attracted investments exceeding 350,000 golden louis.

But Mesmer proved no more popular with the French medical establishment than he had with its counterpart in Austria. The State Medical College set up a Commission of Inquiry in 1784 which eventually issued a scathing report claiming there was nothing in Mesmer's results that couldn't be explained by imagination. It was enough to ruin him. His practice fell away as did the more general interest in 'mesmerism'. He went to Prussia and abandoned medicine completely. He died where he was born, in Swabia, in 1815.

The most interesting thing about all this is that nobody, then or now, doubts the reality of Mesmer's cures. It's only his method – or, more accurately, the theory behind it – that has come into question. The question arises that even if his cures were brought about purely by imagination, why did the Commission of Inquiry not recommend that his imaginative techniques should become part of general medical practice?

But it's by no means certain the Commission's verdict was correct. Since Mesmer's day, we've discovered there really are tidal energies flowing through the human body. They can be detected electrically and manipulated by the needling techniques of Chinese acupuncture. There is some evidence they can also be influenced by magnets, exactly as Mesmer believed, and possibly even by the laying on of hands, which alternative practitioners often claim involves a transfer of energy.

Aside from all this, doctors today are (a little) more kindly disposed towards Mesmer than their 18th century counterparts, not because they accept he may have been right, but because most of them now think, quite wrongly, that his real secret was the use of hypnosis.

Chapter 3

You are feeling sleepy...

During Mesmer's heyday, one of his pupils, the Marquis de Puységur, attempted to bring about healing convulsions in a young shepherd boy whom, for everyone's convenience, he had tied to a tree. The Marquis concentrated hard, then vigorously applied the magnetic passes as he'd been taught, but instead of falling into a fit, the shepherd boy's eyelids drooped and he slumped against his ropes. At the same time, he grew astoundingly amenable to taking orders. Nobody realised it at the time, but de Puysegur had just invented hypnosis.

Or rather, reinvented it. There is evidence that hypnosis was understood and used in Ancient Egypt, Ancient India, Ancient China and possibly Ancient Greece. It was sometimes called 'temple sleep', sometimes *mekhenesis*, which means 'the taking away of responsibility' – a very good description of the hypnotic process.

Most people think the hypnotic trance is a form of sleep[2], but it isn't. It's a very special state in which control of your mind is more or less taken over by the hypnotist. The 'more or less' bit of that sentence refers to your depth of trance. A light trance is marked by a feeling of relaxation, but can otherwise hardly be told apart from the normal waking state except by an expert. If you reach medium level trance, the hypnotist can control your pain levels, reinforce your willpower, make you feel slightly nauseous and so on, but not much more.

It's at deep trance – which can be reached by 10–15% of the population – that things get really interesting. If I can persuade you, just once, to reach deep trance, then your mind is mine. Should you ever feel inclined to take that risk, then this, or something very similar, is what will happen to you when you present yourself for an hypnotic session: first off, whatever you've been expecting, there's no battle of wills. The sinister hypnotist with deep-

2 The word hypnosis, which was coined by a Scottish doctor in the 19th century, comes from the Greek for sleep.

set eyes who forces his victim to submit by the sheer power of his mind only exists in fiction. Instead, you'll be asked to make yourself comfortable, maybe even kick off your shoes. A good hypnotist will answer any questions you may have and try, as best (s)he can, to reassure you about the process.

As the process itself begins, the first thing you're likely to notice is an increasing sense of relaxation. Arms and legs will begin to feel heavy and you'll sink comfortably back in your chair. Your eyes will grow tired and eyelids become heavy. At first they'll flicker and you'll want to blink a lot, but only a little later they'll be so heavy that you'll find it easier to let them close. At this stage you may look as if you're asleep, but you aren't. As you sit there with your eyes closed and your body increasingly relaxed, you know you could open your eyes and stand up at any time, no problem at all, but you really don't want to; and it doesn't matter if you sit here just a little while longer, does it?

Around this time, you may realise the hypnotist's voice has become terribly interesting to you. You concentrate on it, listening carefully to every word.

You may well decide it's a wonderfully attractive voice, very soothing, very reassuring. Quite quickly after this you'll notice that anything other than the hypnotist's voice is becoming less and less important. You know everything that's going on in the room, of course, but somehow it no longer bothers you. If somebody shouted 'Fire!' you'd probably just sit there, listening to that soothing voice and waiting to be told what to do next. Within the next few minutes, you won't even be able to hear anything except the hypnotist's voice. Other sounds literally fade away.

For quite a few people this is about as far as it goes. You're now in a medium trance state (although the chances are you won't think so) and the hypnotist is able to control pain in certain parts of your body, notably your hands, or induce a feeling of lightness in your arm so pronounced that it will actually float in the air of its own accord. But if you are one of the special ones – usually highly intelligent, imaginative and creative – you'll go further.

As the hypnotic trance deepens, you'll find yourself increasingly unable to resist the hypnotist's suggestions ... not that you'll really want to. Your powers of judgement will all but disappear. If, for example, I told you now there was a parrot flying round your head, you would look up, find no such parrot and come to the conclusion that I was either mistaken or telling lies.

But if you were in a deep hypnotic trance when I mentioned the parrot, you would look up to find it was actually there. Your mind, unable to resist the hypnotic suggestion, would rather create a hallucination of a parrot than believe the hypnotist could possibly be wrong.

This, as you may already have worked out, is a dangerous state to be in – especially if you don't know the hypnotist is trustworthy. There's an idea abroad that you can't be made to do anything under hypnosis that runs contrary to your moral principles. It dates back to a 19th century demonstration by the great French neurologist, Jean-Martin Charcot.

While teaching a class of medical students at the University of Paris, Charcot hypnotised a pretty servant girl. In the middle of the demonstration, he was called away and, rather rashly, left the class in charge of one of the students. This young man failed to display the integrity and maturity for which medical students are so widely noted and promptly ordered the hypnotised girl to take all her clothes off. The girl woke from her trance at once and slapped his face.

But the idea that you can always resist an immoral suggestion is nonsense. Back in the 1950s, a perfectly respectable Swedish businessman was persuaded under hypnosis to rob a bank *and murder the cashier*. And in a series of clinical experiments in London during the late 1960s, a volunteer housewife was prepared to throw what she thought to be acid into the face of a lab assistant[3].

The incident in Paris only showed the medical student had a limited grasp of technique. If instead

[3] For most of the trials, a harmless fluid was substituted for the acid. In one, however, a careless scientist forgot to make the switch and the lab assistant had to be treated for acid burns.

of directly ordering the girl to strip, he had first told her she was alone in her bedroom preparing for sleep, she would have undressed without hesitation. The housewife who threw acid in the lab assistant's face was persuaded he was a criminal intent on murdering her child and the acid was the only way to stop him.

So, having entered deep trance, you have placed yourself entirely in the hands of the hypnotist – body and mind. This is something that could go far further than you may possibly imagine.

Chapter 4

Hypnotic powers

Several years ago, I was asked to demonstrate on television how hypnosis could be used to influence body functions that would normally lie outside a person's control. My subject, a sales executive named Leonie, was wired up to monitors that recorded her blood pressure, heart rate, brain waves and something called galvanic skin response, which is the rate at which your skin conducts electricity.

Leonie was nervous and excited about appearing on television – she'd had her hair done specially for the occasion – but I'd worked with her before and knew there would be no problem in persuading her to reach a deep trance level. In point of fact, I'd given her what's called a post-hypnotic trigger.

Most people are relieved to learn they can't be hypnotised against their will[4] ... first time. In normal circumstances, you must cooperate with the hypnotist before trance can be induced (and even then it's not always possible). But once you've cooperated and reached the deep trance level, your hypnotist can build in a trigger, usually based on a word or gesture, that allows you to be hypnotised instantly at any future time ... whether you want it or not.

An honest hypnotist will always ask the subject's permission to build in a trigger of this sort, since once in place the effects can be far-reaching. With Leonie, I had only to make a downward movement of one hand over her eyes for her to fall immediately into a deep trance. The challenge, however, was not merely to hypnotise her, but to demonstrate how far hypnotic control could be taken.

The first part of the demonstration was easy. The presenter of the show needed to be convinced that Leonie was really in trance and not just pretending. A glance at the brainwave monitor gave the proof. In trance, the electrical pattern of

---

[4] Unless drugs or long-term brainwashing techniques like sleep deprivation are used.

your brain is completely different to that of your waking state. By using the trigger to move Leonie in and out of trance at will, the change in brainwaves was very evident. Next came the influence of galvanic skin response, which was even easier. This response changes as you relax. As Leonie dropped into trance, her entire body relaxed profoundly and the skin monitor recorded the change.

So far, the changes were fairly subtle, but the presenter remarked that since he didn't really know very much about skin responses and brainwaves, he still wasn't convinced the subject was really hypnotised. I suggested to Leonie she could no longer feel pain and pushed a sterilised needle through the flesh of her arm. She lay peacefully unaware of what was going on and the presenter admitted that fakery was no longer likely.

Raising her heart rate and blood pressure was no problem at all. Leonie was an enthusiastic motorist. I told her she was driving on the local race-track to win an important trophy. Leonie experienced the event as a full-blown hallucination and her natural excitement drove up both her heart rate and her blood pressure.

Although my ten-minute demonstration with Leonie attracted considerable interest, it hardly began to scratch the surface of the control a hypnotist has over his subject. In one of the first hypnotic demonstrations I ever witnessed, a lightly built man was told his body had become rigid as an iron bar. He was then lifted and laid out between two chairs, the nape of his neck resting on one chair-back, his heels resting on the other. He was able to maintain this position with ease, even when an 88-kilogram man climbed up to stand on his chest.

With a deep trance subject, almost any physical effect becomes possible. A strong man can be made so weak he can scarcely stand, or a weak one turned into an arm-wrestling champion. Pain control can be extended far beyond my little demonstration with Leonie. Surgical amputations have been carried out without anaesthetic, simply by suggesting the patient will feel no pain. During operations of this type, bleeding can be controlled using hypnotic suggestion and the effects of shock reduced to a minimum.

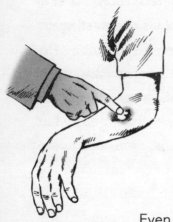

Some effects are downright weird. If, for example, you tell a deeply hypnotised subject you are going to burn him with a red-hot poker, then touch him with your finger, his skin will blister exactly as if you really *had* burned him.

Even more peculiar is the fact that warts can be banished by hypnosis. Warts are caused by a virus and should, in theory, lie well beyond the effects of suggestion. So should the size of a woman's breasts, yet experiments have shown a 5-centimetre increase in the bust measurement of volunteer subjects.

As you lie entranced while all this nonsense is going on, you are not, despite all appearances, deeply asleep. But you might well think you were when the hypnotist finally brings you back to normal consciousness. Because at this point, something called post-hypnotic amnesia cuts in. The term simply means that, unless given suggestions to the contrary, a deeply hypnotised subject will instantly forget everything that happened once the trance is ended. So looking back, it *feels* as if you've been asleep, even though you weren't.

Post-hypnotic amnesia is one of the more dangerous aspects of the deep trance experience, because it means you have no idea what happened to you during the time you were hypnotised. You may have been assaulted or persuaded to stroll stark naked down the high street. You may have given all your money to the dog's home or promised to marry the hypnotist. You'll remember none of it. And that includes any *post*-hypnotic suggestion you've been given.

A post-hypnotic suggestion is an instruction implanted in trance, but only carried out after you've woken up again. The hypnotist might tell you that when you hear a particular sound you'll find your feet have gone on fire or that you're surrounded by fairies or leprechauns. When that sound plays, perhaps days or even weeks later, you'll behave as if what he told you was true. Worse still, you won't be able to stop your reaction.

From all this you'll appreciate that hypnosis is a very powerful tool. But before we find out whether it can really explain Wolf Messing's weird abilities, you need to find out quite how powerful it can be.

Chapter 5

Super memory

How's your maths? How long would it take you to divide 4 by 47 and give me the answer to… oh, let's say six decimal places? No, no – leave your calculator alone and put down that pencil and paper. You have to do this sum in your head, carrying over from memory. It took Professor A. C. Aitken of Edinburgh University just 24 seconds to do that sum in his head; except he didn't stop at six decimal places. "It's point 08510638297872340425531914893617021276595744 68 – and that's the repeating point. It starts again then at 085," he told his questioner.

The professor was known for his extraordinary memory. If you're presented with a list of random numbers, the chances are you'll not be able to remember more than seven of them in sequence.

(You might do a little better or a little worse, but that's the average.) Professor Aitken, on the other hand, could remember 1,000 – that's not a misprint – in the right order without making a single mistake.

If you find that hard to believe, you're going to have real trouble with Rajan Mahadevan. Back in 1981, while he was visiting Mangalore, they asked him the decimal value of pi, the fraction $^{22}/_7$ which represents the ratio of a circle's circumference to its diameter. Mr Mahadevan got himself into the record books by reciting the answer, from memory, to 31,811 decimal places.

It's not just numbers either. Professor Aitken could memorise long passages of text (in both English and Latin) almost instantly and recall them perfectly years later. But even this doesn't come close to the limits of human memory. When the American author Alex Hailey went off to find his ancestral roots in Africa, he discovered there were people who could recite from memory detailed tribal histories, including names and personal events, running back centuries. The complete recitation would often take weeks. Many experts believe this is how we all recorded history before the invention of writing.

In the late 1960s, the Russian psychologist A. R. Luria published an account of 30 years he spent studying a memory artist identified only as 'S'. S seemed literally incapable of forgetting anything. Luria began by giving him enormous lists of numbers which he memorised without problems. Later, Luria started to wonder how long these memories would be retained.

Astoundingly, he discovered that not only could S still remember the number lists after 20 years, but he could also remember what Luria was wearing and what the weather was like when he memorised the lists in the first place.

HOW TO IMPROVE YOUR MEMORY

If you have problems remembering the time of day, here's something that may help. Set yourself up with a locus.

A locus is a place where you put things you want to remember. But it's a place that exists inside your head. To set up your locus, pick a building you know very well – maybe your home, your school or your local library. The bigger it is the better, since you may want to store a great many items there.

Take time to picture the building in your mind. Imagine you're walking through it, room by room. Try to make the daydream as clear and detailed as possible.

When your locus is in place, when, that is, you can close your eyes and easily imagine yourself walking through it, test yourself using this list:

Coin	Teddy bear	Coat
Whip	Statue	Vase
Radio	Banana	Woolly rug
Book	Egyptian Mummy	Beetle
Lollypop	Chainsaw	Teacup
Spectacles	Dentures	Drum kit
Cake	Sword	

There are 20 items there. Turn this book over and see how many you can remember. You'll be lucky if you manage half of them. Now imagine you're leaving each item in your locus: the coin on the doorsteps, the whip in the hallway, the radio on the stairs and so on. Walk through your locus depositing items until you've worked your way completely through the list.

Now close your eyes and walk through the locus again. Write down the items as you find them. See how much better you did this time?

You can even remember long numbers like Professor Aitken using your locus. But you have to convert them into pictures first: 1 = Bun; 2 = Shoe; 3 = Tree; 4 = Door; 5 = Hive; 6 = Sticks; 7 = Heaven; 8 = Gate; 9 = Wine; 0 (zero) = Hero. Leave the numbers in their correct sequence as you walk through your locus, then collect them later by walking through again *in the same way.*

In 1970, the scientific journal *Nature* reported on a man who remembered what appeared to be a pattern of random dots so vividly that he was able mentally to fuse them with a second pattern some time later. The scientists who ran the experiment confirmed this remarkable ability by creating two patterns that showed up a square in the middle when brought together.

Memory masters like this are generally thought of as exceptional – perhaps even freaks whose brains are somehow wired differently from those of the rest of us. Luria's memory artist S certainly had a peculiar mind – he could taste shapes and hear colours, a condition known as synesthesia – although he wasn't actually very bright. But some interesting findings in Canada has shown we may all have the basic equipment to match any memory feat S or Professor Aitken ever managed.

If you ever have to undergo brain surgery, the chances are you won't be given a general anaesthetic. The brain itself has no pain receptors so they can slice into it without you feeling a thing. But more to the point, some brain operations actually require you to be wide awake so you can tell the surgeon exactly what's happening.

This was the case for a patient of Dr Wilder Penfield of the Montreal Neurological Institute. But during her operation, when Dr Penfield touched a particular area of her brain with his scalpel, she suddenly began to report a vivid childhood memory.

Dr Penfield was so intrigued by this that he set up a series of experiments in which he stimulated a specific area of patients' brains with a weak electrical current. Every one, without exception, reported playback of long-forgotten conversations and experiences.

The really interesting thing about these reports was that the memories were complete. It was as if the patients were actually *reliving* what had happened to them[5] complete with associated sounds, emotions, sensations and smells. It seems from all this that we go through life with a tape deck running in our brain, painstakingly recording absolutely everything we ever experience[6].

But if astounding feats of memory are possible and your brain acts like a permanent VCR, how come you can hardly remember what you had for breakfast? The plain fact is that with a little help from your friendly neighbourhood hypnotist ... you can!

[5] Although they knew they weren't. Several claimed it was like being in two places at the same time: one was the operating table with its wires in their brain, the other was the place they were remembering.

[6] It's interesting to wonder why this may be so. Why have we been created as walking recording machines? What are we going to do with this information? And when?

When the medical profession began to take hypnosis seriously back in the 19th century, an endless stream of reports appeared detailing how it could be used to improve memory, sometimes to a remarkable degree. There are cases on record of subjects able to speak fluently languages they had not used for up to 50 years and firmly believed they had forgotten.

There were even examples of difficult, perhaps shocking, childhood memories recalled under hypnosis, but promptly forgotten again in the waking state. This peculiarity was noted by the founder of psychoanalysis, Dr Sigmund Freud, who, in the early days of his practice, used hypnosis extensively to help patients remember past experiences and hence understand themselves better.

Hypnosis is still used by 21st century psychiatrists in much the same way, but research has shown super memory is the least of the strange powers it can unlock.

Sigmund Freud

Chapter 6

Weird talents

These days it's not very fashionable for scientists to believe in psychic abilities, so experiments to test them are seldom carried out. Things were different in the 19th century. Open-minded scientists were curious about psychical phenomena, with the result that more work was done in the field and a large body of evidence built up – much of it with the aid of hypnosis.

Some of the talents displayed while in trance were weird indeed. A Swedish doctor named Agardh described the case of a 15-year-old patient who developed a remarkable degree of clairvoyance (the ability to know things that are not usually detected by the normal senses)[7]. For example, the boy could correctly name the title

[7] Oddly enough, it only really began to show itself after the boy survived a serious illness.

and describe the contents of any book placed against his chest.

Dr Agardh experimented by having him read a letter with his eyes closed. Then, lest the boy was somehow cheating, he was required to read a *folded* letter with his eyes closed. He displayed his powers frequently outside of formal tests. On one occasion he told a woman – correctly – that she was pregnant, although she herself had no idea at the time. On another he was able to tell at once that a specially constructed ring contained a second ring hidden inside it.

A French subject named Alexis Didier was one of dozens who seemed able to discover information under hypnosis that it was impossible for them to know. When an army man named Captain Daniel asked Didier to describe his (Daniel's) father's house, Didier launched into a description that included painstaking details of furnishings, pictures, ornaments and even the position of doors and windows. Captain Daniel was impressed. He said that throughout the entire session, Didier only made one mistake – he got the colour of the curtains wrong. But when the good Captain visited his father's home after the experiment, he discovered Didier had been right about the curtains after all.

Early records of hypnosis are packed with reports of this type. One common experiment was to suggest to subjects that they could taste things the hypnotist put in his own mouth. Time and again, the subjects' 'guesses' proved correct. But nowhere did hypnosis trigger psychical talent more strongly than in the case of America's famous 'sleeping prophet', Edgar Cayce.

Edgar was born in 1877 on a Kentucky farmstead. His parents were both devout Christians and he grew up to be a reserved, religious, scholarly boy. But at the age of seven, he suddenly told his parents that he'd just had a conversation with his grandfather. It was a more worrying announcement than it sounds: his grandfather had been dead for some time. Later, young Edgar reported he'd been talking to an angel.

Today there are a lot of myths surrounding the name of Edgar Cayce. One is that he was able to 'read' an entire book just by laying his head on it and falling asleep. He certainly had a great love of books and at age 16 actually took a job in a bookshop. But like most normal boys he liked sport and, this being America, played baseball. During one game, Cayce was struck violently by a ball in his back. He collapsed and had to be carried off the field. On-the-spot first aid did nothing for the pain and a local doctor ordered him to take to bed. But that didn't work either and Cayce lay for days in agony.

Then, out of the blue, he asked his mother to make a particular type of poultice (soothing mixture spread on a bandage) and apply it to the affected area. She did as he asked and the next morning the pain had gone. But when she asked him where he found out how to make the poultice, he couldn't remember telling her anything. It seems likely from this account that young Edgar was showing the first faint signs of psychism, but it

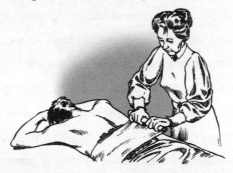

took another five years – and the application of hypnosis – before his talent really began to flower.

By this time, Cayce had left his bookshop job to take up another post as a salesman for a wholesale stationery company. Everything went well until he developed a sore throat and lost his voice. For some reason the condition refused to get better. Most of the time he could only talk in a whisper – a useless situation for a salesman – and he soon found himself out of a job.

Cayce went from doctor to doctor looking for a cure. When none could help, he got desperate and consulted a local hypnotist. Interestingly, hypnosis eased his symptoms a little, but didn't result in a cure. The hypnotist told him the problem was he couldn't induce a deep enough level of trance. Cayce decided to try another hypnotist.

The decision proved a turning point not only in his condition, but also in his life. The man he picked was Al Layne, somebody as interested in healing and mysticism as he was in hypnosis. Layne examined Cayce, heard the story of the earlier attempts at treatment and came to the conclusion that the case needed an unorthodox approach.

Layne figured that even if the doctors didn't know what was wrong with Cayce, Cayce's own subconscious mind was bound to. So he decided that rather than suggesting Cayce's voice should come back (as the first hypnotist had done) he would instead suggest Cayce should describe the cause of his affliction ... and prescribe his own cure. What happened next was creepy. Cayce fell into a deep, hypnotic trance almost at once and to Layne's astonishment the whisper disappeared immediately.

"We see the body," Cayce said in a clear, strong voice, using for the first time an expression that was to become his trademark in years to come. He then went on to talk in detail about the cause of his throat problem, which, he said, was the result of poor blood circulation causing a deficiency of the nerves in the area. What was needed for a cure was an improvement in circulation. Once that happened, the nerves would quickly recover and the throat would return to normal.

Like most hypnotists, Layne was very aware of how well simple bodily processes react to suggestion so he told Cayce that the blood circulation in his neck was beginning to increase. Moments later he could see the reddening of the skin as Cayce's body responded. Layne kept up the suggestions for a time, then woke Cayce up. For the first time in months, his throat was pain-free and he could talk normally.

Although it was exactly the result he'd hoped for, Layne was perplexed. The cure went a lot further than the current theories of hypnosis and the subconscious mind allowed. He began to wonder if some sort of outside presence was involved – in other words whether Cayce had been taken over by a spirit. There was a worldwide fad for Spiritualism (contacting the dead through mediums) at the time and while mediums weren't hypnotised, they *did* go into trance and permitted spirits to speak through them.

So Layne decided to put his theory to the test. Cayce's subconscious might just possibly be able to cure Cayce's own ailments, but something else had to be involved if Cayce could do the same for other people. He asked Cayce to give it a try and Cayce, after some initial doubts, saw his first patient on March 31, 1901. It was the beginning of something absolutely extraordinary.

In the early days, Layne hypnotised Cayce before he started each consultation, but this was a complicated procedure and Cayce eventually learned how to hypnotise himself. Henceforth, he would allow himself to relax and quickly sink into trance. Then, typically, he would say, "Yes, we see the body," and begin a detailed report of what was wrong with the patient.

Often the root causes he discovered for his clients' illnesses were far from obvious. He might speak about lesions resulting from childhood illnesses, to spinal misadjustments, to malfunctions of the glands. The cures he prescribed were equally unpredictable – the records show he once suggested a patient make use of 'bed-bug juice'.

Eccentric or not, his approach worked,

sometimes miraculously well. By the time he died in 1945, Edgar Cayce had diagnosed and treated an estimated 22,000 patients and accumulated literally thousands of grateful testimonials to his healing skills. All because of the remarkable talent hypnosis managed to unlock in him.

But it was in Russia, not America that serious scientists worked to show how far-reaching hypnosis could be when it came to releasing talents.

Chapter 7

Artificial reincarnation

Picture the scene. It's Moscow, 1966. The Soviet Union is still one of the world's two great superpowers. Most forms of religious practice have been banned and even scientific research is under State control. Nobody has any time for woolly theories about hypnosis and the power of the mind. Yet a journalist from *Pravda*, Russia's largest newspaper, was about to stumble on a story so spooky as to be almost unbelievable.

Comrade A. Tsipko, the journalist in question, was on a tour of a particular educational establishment, one that was doing well, getting results, but was the subject of rumours about the mysterious nature of its methods. Tsipko's guide was Dr Vladimir L. Raikov, a soberly dressed individual with a curiously reassuring presence.

Together they entered a studio room, already deep in conversation as the journalist tried to find out more about the institution he was visiting. Several young students were already in the room, apparently engaged in an art class: they were drawing a life model posed in the sunlight from a large picture window.

Dr Raikov offered to introduce his star pupil. A girl in her early twenties stepped forward to shake Tsipko's hand. "My name is Raphael," she said. "Raphael of Urbino." Tsipko blinked. Raphael of Urbino, master painter and architect of the Italian renaissance, died on April 6, 1520 ... more than 400 years before.

Tsipko questioned the girl carefully. Although she appeared perfectly normal, it seemed that she believed herself to be a man living in the year 1505.

Nothing in the modern world affected her. When Tsipko produced a camera, she had no idea what it was and denied having seen anything like it in her life. When he tried to talk to her about things like telephones or aeroplanes, she became increasingly disturbed until finally she screamed at him that he was talking nonsense.

Dr Raikov was a psychiatrist by profession. Was this one of his patients, a lunatic who believed herself to be the man who created some of the greatest artworks of the Vatican? The thought must have passed through Tsipko's head, but the truth was far stranger. "That was an example of what we call artificial reincarnation," Dr Raikov told him.

There's an hypnotic technique known as *regression* by which subjects are persuaded to recall what appear to be memories of past lives, but while Raikov was a master hypnotist, what he was talking about turned out to be very different. The psychiatrist had, in fact, developed an approach to teaching students that almost involved calling on the spirits of dead masters to help them out.

The process is illustrated by the case of Alla, who was, in the 1960s, a promising physics student at Moscow University. She had no interest in art and precious little talent for it either. Any time she tried to draw, the result was matchstick figures with no life, form or feeling.

When Alla volunteered to help Dr Raikov with his experiments, the first thing he did was test how thoroughly she could be hypnotised. Experience had shown him he could only produce the artificial reincarnation effect in subjects able to reach deep trance levels. Indeed in some of his papers he hinted that he was making use of a whole new type of active trance.

Even today, the curious area of active trance is seldom investigated and not very well understood. But to judge from the reports, what Dr Raikov did was to hypnotise his subjects in the usual way, then, when deep trance was established, he would switch from instructing them to relax to telling them they were becoming more and more alert.

Active Trance

Monitoring subjects' brain waves using a machine called an electroencephalograph (EEG for short) shows the artificial reincarnation trance is very different to the deep hypnotic trance that leads into it.

In normal hypnosis, the brain produces an alpha pattern indicating that the subject is deeply relaxed, although not actually asleep. In the reincarnation trance, the alpha pattern disappeared altogether and the brain waves showed the subjects have become unusually alert and highly focused. It's as if their entire attention was trained like a laser on the new personality that has taken them over.

Dr Raikov also tested subjects using a newly developed electronic machine that measured electrical energies flowing through the acupuncture channels of their bodies. This too confirmed that while in the reincarnation trance they had entered a state of 'super wakefulness' quite different to ordinary hypnotic trance.

All the same, subjects did forget their experiences afterwards, exactly as they would in hypnosis, and often fell into a deep sleep when passing from the reincarnation trance to ordinary consciousness.

The result of this approach is a highly energised, eyes-open mindset that most subjects find pleasant and invigorating. They appear to be wide awake and are capable of looking after themselves, but despite appearances, they are not in their normal state of consciousness and are just as open to suggestions from the hypnotist as they would be in the more familiar form of passive trance.

In any case, once Alla reached the required trance level, Dr Raikov told her firmly she was Ilya Yefimovich Repin, a Russian painter of historical subjects who died in 1930. Although some of his most famous work dated to before the 1917 Communist Revolution when the Russian Tsar was overthrown, Repin was much admired in the Soviet Union.

Raikov went on to suggest to Alla that she thought exactly like Repin, saw the world exactly like Repin and had all Repin's immense talent at her fingertips. He then induced the active form of trance that allowed the girl to live as Repin, at least within the safety of his institute. Every few days, he reinforced the basic suggestion: Alla was no longer Alla – she was now the famous painter Ilya Repin.

The result of this approach was remarkable. The girl who had only been able to draw matchstick men when she arrived quickly began to exhibit genuine artistic talent. Those around her could see improvements on a daily basis. After just ten days living as the artificially reincarnated Repin, she had developed such an interest in art that she took to carrying a sketchpad everywhere.

Dr Raikov varied his approach by calling Raphael into Alla, exactly as he'd done with the student he introduced to the man from *Pravda*. (Presumably he kept the two 'Raphaels' apart to avoid conflict.) But most of the time she functioned as Repin. In fact she lived as Repin for three months, at the end of which she was able to draw like a professional and seriously considered giving up physics in favour of art.

In an experiment, Dr Raikov and his colleagues incarnated various artists in the bodies of some 20 students, most of them in their late teens. Like Alla, they lived as these artists for periods of up to three months. None of the subjects turned into master painters, nor did they develop styles anything like those of their reincarnated artists. But all showed noticeable improvement in their artistic talent, even though *how much* they improved differed from subject to subject.

Throughout the early stages of the experiment, awakened subjects couldn't remember their activities during the reincarnation trance. Even when shown the pictures they'd painted, they didn't recognise their own work. But after about the tenth session, they began to realise they could draw and paint a lot better than they used to, even in their normal waking state. In other words, their natural talent had increased.

The Raikov experiments weren't confined to reincarnating painters. One subject found her personality changed to that of an historical English queen. Another became a sequence of children of various ages. But by far the most interesting development came when he used artificial reincarnation to cure a serious medical condition.

Dr Raikov treated a well-educated, middle-aged patient named Boris who was a chronic alcoholic. Like many others with the problem, Boris would work hard to give up liquor, then break down and go on a drinking spree, which was then followed by periods of great remorse ... until he went off the rails again. By the time Boris came to see Dr Raikov, the pattern had repeated far too often and his family were on the point of leaving him.

Raikov began by taking a full psychiatric history of his patient, during which he discovered that Boris viewed his mother with particular warmth and affection. Realising that the standard psychiatric approaches to alcoholism have a poor success record, he decided to try a bizarre experiment based on his experience with artificial reincarnation: he determined to reincarnate Boris *as his own mother*.

The experiment went well. When Dr Raikov asked the entranced Boris who he was, he promptly replied, "Tatyana Nikolaevna," – his mother's name. After several tests to ensure the new personality was firmly in place, Raikov told the 'woman' that her son was lying on the couch, turning blue in a drunken stupor.

Boris reacted exactly as his own mother would have in such circumstances. He threw himself on the empty couch and attempted artificial respiration in an attempt to revive the drunken 'son.' Acting through Boris's body, Tatyana begged the doctor to help her give first aid, then berated her son for drinking so much.

Dr Raikov increased the pressure. He poured water loudly into a glass and told Tatyana her son seemed to be drinking again. Boris/Tatyana promptly grabbed the invisible bottle from her invisible son and smashed it on the ground.

Encouraged by the initial results, Raikov reincarnated Boris's daughter, who told her father tearfully that it was terrible for her when he drank. This was followed by reincarnations of the man's wife and other family members, all of whom expressed their horror at his drinking habits.

Although the treatment was marked by tears and some violent outbursts of emotion, Boris remembered absolutely nothing about it when he was awakened from the reincarnation trance. On the face of it, nothing seemed to have changed, then, days later, Boris told Raikov he had begun to realise how his family must feel about his drinking. "It's horrifying," he said. "I've decided to quit."

In one of his rare interviews granted to Western writers, Dr Raikov suggested his artificial reincarnation techniques might be used to rehabilitate criminals by letting them discover how their activities were viewed by their victims.

Certainly he has shown that his approach can do more than stimulate drawing talent. On one occasion he reincarnated the persona of Fritz Kreisler, a famous violinist, in a student at the Moscow Conservatory of Music ... and a dramatic increase in performance followed. On another, he reincarnated a mathematical genius in the body of a college maths student. The boy's grades promptly improved.

Raikov's most intriguing experiment, however, came when he hypnotised a Russian aeronautics engineer and told him he was an (unnamed) famous inventor from the distant future, someone capable of designing spaceships that could reach the stars. The reincarnated inventor agreed and set to drawing up plans. Raikov filed away the blueprints carefully against the day when science might (hopefully) be advanced enough to understand them.

But for all the ingenuity of Dr Raikov's work, nothing in it comes close to explaining Wolf Messing's weird abilities. Raikov began by hypnotising his subjects in the usual way and even the later change in trance type did not produce the sort of results Messing managed. In fact, from everything we've seen so far it would appear that if Messing used hypnosis at all, he must have used it in a form wholly new to anything we've seen so far.

Perhaps the answer lies in a chance remark Messing himself made when asked to explain how he penetrated the security of Stalin's dacha: "I walked through mentally broadcasting the message 'I am Beria... I am Beria,'" he said. Lavrenti Beria was the hated head of the Soviet Secret Police and a frequent visitor to the dacha. Was it possible that Messing (who looked nothing like Beria) could instantly convince dozens of guards that he was someone he was not? Was it possible he somehow *reached into their minds?*

Chapter 8

The Willing Game

Back in the mid 1870s, a craze for something called 'The Willing Game' swept through America and Britain. For a while it seemed as if the game was being played in every living room in the land. It was an addiction to match the hula hoop, Rubik's Cube or reading Harry Potter.

The way the game played out was simple – so simple you can easily try it out for yourself: all you need is a group of interested friends. One member of a group would leave the room while the others decided among themselves on an object he would be willed to find or some action he would be willed to carry out.

When the person returned, the group would silently command him to take the appropriate action. Amazingly, he would very often perform exactly as required, sometimes remarkably quickly. The effect was dramatically increased if a member of the group took his hand or touched his shoulder. To make sure there was no cheating, each member of the group would take his or her turn at being the subject. Some proved better than others, but the game worked well enough overall to be a fascinating and diverting pastime. The question that concerned many people at the time was how the game worked.

One popular theory was that muscle-reading was involved, the sort of thing described in the first chapter of this book. This seems reasonable enough when the subject was willed to find a particular object and a member of the group was touching him, but certainly wouldn't explain those times when the subject wasn't touched, or when he was willed to carry out a particular action, like touching his nose or scratching his ear. In 1875, a paper published in the *Detroit Review of Medicine* seriously suggested 'thought-transference' was involved.

Much the same idea occurred to the Reverend A. M. Creery of Buxton in Britain. He took to playing The Willing Game with his four daughters and quickly discovered that they could do a lot more than pick up objects or carry out simple actions. Time and again they could tell exactly what the group was concentrating on, like the names of people or towns. He tested them by having the group think of cards drawn at random from a deck and even, on occasion, lines of poetry. The girls did so well he decided to have their abilities professionally investigated.

The man he chose for the job was William Barrett, a Professor of Physics at the Royal College of Science in Dublin, who had a special interest in the subject for a very odd reason. Barrett had been involved with a friend in a series of experiments with Mesmerism – the old original 'animal magnetism' style of Mesmerism, not the later hypnotism – using children from an Irish village.

During the course of these experiments, Barrett noted one girl seemed to show an astonishing ability to pick up information while in trance by mysterious means. He persuaded his friend (who was the mesmerist on these occasions) to test the girl scientifically.

Between them, they set up test conditions that ensured the girl could not possibly see what was happening, then, when she'd been placed in trance, the mesmerist held his hand over a lighted lamp. The girl snatched her own hand back with a gasp as if it had been burned. The mesmerist placed a sugar cube in his mouth. The girl sucked on an invisible cube in her own mouth with an expression of pleasure. The mesmerist placed a bitter substance on his tongue. The girl grimaced.

So it went on. By the time the tests were finished, Barrett had concluded this was not the heightened sense perceptions well recognised by scientists investigating hypnosis, but something that involved what he called a 'community of sensation'. And it wasn't just that the girl seemed to be experiencing the same *physical* sensations as her mesmerist – she also seemed able to pick up his ideas and emotions as well.

What Barrett was talking about was telepathy. When he investigated the Creery children, he decided they were displaying it as well and wrote a short report for the scientific magazine *Nature*. Barrett's findings were confirmed by further tests carried out by several members of the newly formed Society for Psychical Research. These tests were analysed by a statistician who concluded the odds against guesswork by the girls were in the region of 9,999,999,999,999,999,999,999,999,999,999 to 1.

Telepathy in Life

It's probably fair to say most people believe they've experienced telepathy at least once in their lives.

How often have you been thinking about a particular friend when the phone rings and you find you're talking to them? The same thing sometimes happens in the street when you find yourself thinking about someone you haven't seen in years, then turn the corner to see them walking towards you. One scientist, Rupert Sheldrake, has conducted experiments that show pets often know by telepathy when their owners decide to come home.

You can even test telepathy for yourself by staring fixedly at the back of someone's neck. Often you'll find they become uneasy and turn round.

There have been many reported instances of telepathy throughout history, including several mentioned in the Bible. Jesus knew the woman of Samaria had had five husbands without being told (John 4: 18). In the Old Testament, the Prophet Elisha could be relied on to tell what the King of Syria was planning in his war against the Israelites (Second Kings 6: 8–12).

Sometimes instances of telepathy can

be very spectacular. In one (quite typical) case study, a woman woke suddenly one morning convinced that she'd received a violent blow to the mouth and her upper lip was bleeding badly.

Moments later, she realised it had all been a dream – her mouth was undamaged and there was no bleeding. But her husband, who was out sailing, was struck by the tiller at the exact moment the woman had woken from her dream. His mouth was hurt and his top lip bled profusely.

A few years later, the British philosophers Malcolm Guthrie and James Birchall carried out a series of controlled experiments on two showroom assistants who had something of a reputation as psychics. The women, referred to in the reports as 'Miss J' and 'Miss E', were blindfold and required to name various objects the experimenters were looking at out of their range of vision.

The results were encouraging. Miss J correctly identified an egg and a playing card, then went on to describe a coin as something 'like a flat, bright button', a gold earring as 'round, bright and yellow with a loop to hang it by,' and a pen holder with a thimble popped over the end as 'a column with something bell-shaped turned upside down on it'.

Further tests of the same two young women showed they were equally skilled at picking up tastes. One of them was able to tell when the experimenter was tasting cloves, a boiled sweet and bitter aloes. She described candied ginger as 'something sweet and hot'. But perhaps the most impressive results arose when Miss E was asked to duplicate a series of drawings telepathically. Her efforts were strikingly close to the originals in almost every case, as the illustration here clearly shows:

Originals

Telepathic drawings

You'd imagine work like this would have been more than enough to establish the reality of telepathy, but scientists then (and now) disliked the idea so much that they demanded more proof. Dr Horatio Donkin, a physician at the Westminster Hospital, published an article in which he insisted that the only way such tests could be taken seriously was if, 'the good faith of the individuals concerned should form no part of the data on which the conclusion is to rest' – a polite way of saying the experimenters had to show they weren't cheating or lying through their teeth.

The honesty of physicists, chemists and other such hard-working scientists had never been questioned in this way and it's difficult to see how any experimenter, in any discipline, could prove absolutely that he wasn't making up his data[9]. But despite the insulting criticism, the psychical researchers pressed on with their experiments.

In the two years that followed, the Society for Psychical Research analysed the results of 17 telepathic trials in which various subjects tried to guess which suit – spades, clubs, diamonds, hearts – was turned up from a pack of playing cards out of

[9] It's no good getting witnesses to watch your experiments. The hardened sceptic simply claims you're all working in collusion or that you're fooling them with clever tricks.

their sight. In the majority of these trials, more than 1,000 guesses were made, yet the calculated odds against chance in the final results worked out at around 1,000,000,000 to 1.

It still wasn't enough for the scientific disbelievers. By now they'd begun to make something of a religion out of denying results that upset current theories. One of their number, Albert Moll, conducted a striking series of experiments in which subjects (hypnotised, as it happened) were asked to pick out glasses of water or specific playing cards that had been 'magnetised' by Moll making mesmeric passes over them.

Moll was a careful man. He even went so far as to cover the items with a sheet of glass in case the subject might be able to pick up the tiny residue of heat from his hands. Despite all precautions, some subjects proved perfectly capable of spotting the correct items.

In one case, he set out to fool a subject by *pretending* a particular card had been magnetised while actually magnetising another. She went straight to the pretend card. A more perceptive scientist might have begun to wonder whether 'magnetism' had anything to do with the results –

it certainly looked as though this subject at least was tuning in to his intent rather than any direct influence on the card. Indeed *all* the successful results might have been explained by telepathy.

But Moll would have none of it. Even when commenting on the experiments carried out by Malcolm Guthrie where he admitted he could find no fault whatsoever with the test conditions, Moll said he was convinced that some sources of error must have been overlooked.

This sort of attitude plagued psychical research at the time[10], but the day eventually came when a scientist emerged who was determined to structure his experiments so carefully and analyse the results so rigorously that the sceptics would no longer have anything to complain about. He was an American and his name was Joseph Banks Rhine.

An ex-Marine who began his professional career as a research botanist, Dr Rhine and his wife Louise both joined the Department of Psychology at Duke University in North Carolina in 1927 and very quickly turned their attention to paranormal investigation. (Ten years later they set up the

[10] And still does, by and large, to this day.

world's first Parapsychology Laboratory at the university.)

Although Rhine started out by investigating the tricky questions of communication through mediums and life after death, he soon developed a new approach to the whole question of psychical research. He was interested in the card-guessing experiments that had already been carried out in Britain, but realised that they had certain built-in flaws that made their results a bit suspect. For example, many people are superstitious about the ace of spades, a card associated with death, and would sometimes unconsciously avoid mentioning it during a test. There are 52 cards in a standard deck, two colours (red or black) and four suits (spades, hearts, diamonds, clubs.) This means you have one chance in two of guessing a card's colour, one chance in four of guessing its suit, and just one chance in 52 of guessing the actual card itself. Statistics like these form the base-line against which psychism has to be measured. But if people unconsciously avoid certain cards, it throws out the statistics, so you never get a true baseline.

So Rhine asked his colleague Karl Zener to design a new pack of cards that would have no bad associations for anybody. He responded by creating a special symbol deck containing 25 cards, five cards each featuring a cross, a square, a circle, wavy lines or a star. These cards, appropriately enough called a Zener pack, have now become a standard tool of psychical research.

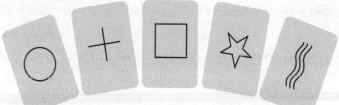

A Zener deck looks simple, but if you ever use one you'll quickly come to realise how very clever it actually is. With five different cards, all equally represented in the pack, a subject has one chance in five of calling any card correctly by sheer guesswork. That means chance will deliver an average of five correct calls in every run of the pack. (Since four runs of the pack make a test of 100 guesses – 4x25=100 – all you have to do is multiply by four to get the percentage – 20%.) But if somebody consistently gets an average score that is different from five in every run of the pack, you can be sure there's something at work over and above chance. Rhine called this 'something' ESP, which stands for Extra Sensory Perception and covers a variety of talents ... including telepathy.

When Rhine started to work with these cards, the results were little short of amazing. One subject, a young student called Hubert Pearce, averaged nine correct guesses per run over a series of 15 runs, giving odds against chance of 100,000,000,000,000,000,000 to 1.

Although several of Rhine's fellow scientists insulted and abused him when he finally published his findings, patient experimentation with increasingly tighter controls has gone a long way towards convincing the scientific community that the reality of telepathy has now been soundly established.

This being so, Wolf Messing's claim that he mentally broadcast the message *I am Beria* begins to make a little sense. But it doesn't explain everything. Even if Messing had somehow perfected the art of sending his thoughts to other people – perhaps whole groups of people at the same time – it's difficult to understand why these people should accept the thought as true.

Beria was a familiar figure. Messing bore no resemblance to him. It would have only needed a passing glance to convince Stalin's guards that the thought which occurred to them was nonsense. There had to be some other factor involved.

Chapter 9

Mind control

Years ago, when I was working as a newspaper editor, a middle-aged man presented himself at my office with an interesting – and disturbing – story.

He had left his home country as a young man and emigrated to Canada. He'd done well in Canada and eventually moved from there to the suburbs of a small town in the United States where he set up his own dry cleaning business. This too prospered to the point where he was thinking of expanding, but one day as he was about to close for the night, he noticed a strange man standing at the street corner watching him.

It was the start of something very nasty. The watcher was back the following day and the day after. Sometimes he stayed at the street corner, sometimes he came closer to the dry cleaning shop and peered through the window. After a few weeks other watchers joined him.

The man in my office – I'll call him Joe for convenience, although that's not his real name – told me that at this point he began to think he was under surveillance by the FBI (Federal Bureau of Investigation) who may have suspected him of some crime because he was an immigrant.

Towards the end of the month, Joe could stand it no longer. The next time he spotted the watcher on the corner, he left his business, walked right up to him and demanded to know what he was doing. The watcher simply turned and walked away.

For a little while, Joe thought his direct action had done the trick. Although he paid careful attention, the people watching him all seemed to have disappeared. He thought the FBI might have decided he was no threat to the community after all. But then the mind control started.

Joe told me he thought the authorities were using some sort of advanced electronic machines for the job, but he didn't really know. All he did know was that somebody out there was taking over his thoughts. Whoever did it had complete access to his mind. Joe could be made to think anything they wanted, imagine things they wanted him to imagine. Some of the pictures they put into his mind were disgusting, but there was nothing at all he could do about them.

Gradually the control strengthened until the FBI were able to take over his actions as well as his thoughts. He found himself doing things he didn't want to do and when on one occasion he used willpower to resist, the agents responded by blinding him in one eye, using a ray device.

I asked Joe if he'd thought of looking for help. He said that at first he was afraid because the FBI knew every move he made, but later he became so desperate that he went to the local doctor, who referred him to a psychiatrist.

The psychiatrist decided he was schizophrenic and began a course of treatment that failed to stop the mind control. After nearly eight months of horror, Joe took matters into his own hands. He sold his business, packed his clothes and left the United States for good. To his immense relief, the FBI lost interest and the mind control stopped. No-one was watching him now, no-one was controlling his thoughts or actions and his only reminder of the bad times was his one milky eye.

At the time Joe told me the story, I agreed with his American psychiatrist. The man was clearly schizophrenic whose persecution had probably been stopped by the medical treatment, whatever Joe himself believed. Today I wouldn't be quite so quick to judge. What's changed is that I've discovered mind control really is possible.

The earliest recorded example dates back to Marquis de Puységur, the pupil of Mesmer who accidentally hypnotised the shepherd boy while trying to magnetise him. In subsequent experiments, the Marquis discovered that his entranced subjects were sometimes as susceptible to suggestions uttered mentally as those spoken aloud.

One subject in particular, a girl named Madeline, was particularly sensitive and could be made to walk, sit or pick up a specific object, all on purely mental commands. De Puységur was even able to pass control of Madeline to others. Once he did so, she obeyed their mental commands as well.

Telepathic commands to hypnotised subjects take us another step closer to solving the mystery of Wolf Messing's strange power. But we're not there yet. Clearly Messing could not have gone round every guard at Stalin's dacha carefully hypnotising him ready to receive mental commands when Messing wanted to enter. But if it's possible to *command* hypnotised subjects by telepathy, could it also be possible to *hypnotise* them by telepathy in the first place?

That's precisely the thought that occurred to six academics at a dinner party in 1886. Among those around the table were Professor Pierre Janet, a prominent French psychologist who recommended the use of hypnosis for mental disorders; Frederick Myers, who founded the British Society for Psychical Research and is the man credited with inventing the word 'telepathy', the psychologist Julian Ochorovicz and a doctor named J. H. A. Gilbert. All four were noted for their interest in the paranormal.

At the time, Dr Gilbert had been involved in a series of experiments with a peasant woman named Léonie who, he discovered, could be hypnotised simply by pressing her hand ... but only if Gilbert concentrated. This led to the idea that it wasn't so much the hand pressure that counted, but some sort of 'thought pressure' generated by Gilbert. He put it to the test and found he could hypnotise Léonie by thought alone – no physical contact was necessary.

Intrigued by Dr Gilbert's story, the men at the dinner party began to discuss whether it might be possible for the doctor to hypnotise Léonie by telepathy there and then, despite the fact she wasn't even in the house where they were dining. Gilbert agreed to try and went off to his study to concentrate. The remaining five academics hurried off to surround Léonie's home, which was about a kilometre away.

What happened next was both funny and frightening. As the five men skulked in the shadows, Léonie suddenly emerged from her house with her eyes tight shut and walked briskly to her garden gate. Then, for no apparent reason, she stopped, turned and walked back in again. The men later discovered that just at that point Dr Gilbert allowed his concentration to waver and dozed off. (Ochorovicz remarked unkindly that this was due to the unaccustomed strain of thinking.)

The men waited, but when nothing happened after a few minutes they had a whispered consultation and Pierre Janet was elected to find out what was going on. He walked cautiously up the path to the house, but as he reached the front door it was flung open suddenly and he was almost knocked down by Léonie as she came out, walking very quickly. (Dr Gilbert had woken up again.)

The five scholars regrouped and set off in hot pursuit. Although her eyes were again shut, she somehow managed to avoid lamp-posts and negotiate traffic for fully ten minutes as she headed in the general direction of Dr Gilbert's home. But then she stopped dead and looked around with every sign of confusion. (Dr Gilbert had decided the experiment was a failure and started a game of billiards to amuse himself.)

The watchers decided not to interfere and after a short time, Léonie fell into trance again and continued on her hurried journey. (Dr Gilbert resolved to give the experiment another try, abandoned his billiards and began to concentrate again.)

The conclusion of the experiment was equally bizarre. With renewed confidence that something was happening, Gilbert went to his front door to see if Léonie was coming. As he opened it, she walked into him with such force that she knocked him to the ground. With her eyes still shut, she actually walked over him and ran through the house shouting, "Where is he? Where is he?"

Dr Gilbert picked himself up and called to her mentally. Léonie heard and answered him. This spectacular example of telepathic hypnosis is not the only one on record. Intrigued by what he'd seen, Professor Janet experimented with Léonie and found that he too could place her in trance from the other side of Le Havre just by thinking of her. And like Gilbert, he could call her to him.

Nearly a century later, during the Cold War (when tension between the two superpowers, USA and the Soviet Union mounted), Russian scientists experimented successfully with telepathic hypnosis in the hope of influencing American politicians at a distance. Dr Edward Naumov, a Soviet parapsychologist, recorded an experiment in which a volunteer was successfully commanded to fall ten times out of ten using telepathy. Eight times out of the ten he fell in the specific direction commanded.

After reading the Russian reports, I decided to

try the technique myself and succeeded twice with the same subject (coincidentally also called Leonie but spelled without the accent) whom I'd hypnotised for the television demonstration. She seemed ideal for the experiment.

On the first occasion, I began the mental trance induction while she was sunbathing. It was exactly as if I'd spoken aloud. Her eyes began to flicker, then closed as her body relaxed with all the signs of her having entered trance. I waited for a few moments, then mentally commanded her to wake up. Her eyes opened at once.

It was not an ideal experiment as several of my professional colleagues pointed out when I reported the results. It was a warm summer's day, Leonie was relaxed to begin with and, as a good hypnotic subject, might have fallen spontaneously into trance lulled by the droning of the bees. This would not explain the successful wake-up call, of course, but I decided to repeat the experiment under different circumstances.

The setting was a rowdy party in Leonie's own home. Loud music was playing and the room was packed. I went to the door, stood with my back to Leonie (who was seated on a couch at the time) and began the mental induction process.

After a moment there was a commotion behind me. I turned to find Leonie on the floor, having slipped, apparently unconscious, from the couch. Concerned party-goers were clustered around her trying to wake her up. I waited long enough to ensure these attempts were not proving effective, then mentally ordered Leonie to stand up and shake hands with the person nearest her. This she did to his complete consternation. I then mentally ordered her to open her eyes and return to normal consciousness. Afterwards I discovered she had slipped into trance mid-sentence while talking to a friend seated beside her on the couch.

From all this, it's quite clear that Wolf Messing may have used telepathic hypnosis on at least some of the guards at Stalin's dacha. With suitable hypnotic subjects, he could mentally have placed them in trance, then created the illusion that he was Beria through telepathic suggestion. But there are cases that show for some people mind control can go even further than this.

Chapter 10

Beyond hypnosis

Maria Milheiras met Manuel Nascimento de Melo on January 31, 1985. It was lunchtime and Maria was walking home after a morning spent cleaning a flat near Notting Hill Gate in London. Manuel approached her, tears streaming down his face, and asked her if she was Portuguese. Maria was indeed Portuguese – she and her husband had moved to Britain many years before. When she nodded, Manuel – a man of about 60 – asked her for directions to the clinic of a Dr John Smith. Maria had worked in the district for ten years, but had to tell him she'd never heard of the clinic.

But Manuel launched into a tearful story. His father, he said, had worked in the clinic many years before. One day, while moving a patient from a bed, he found £3,000 in cash beneath the pillow. It was a small fortune in those days. Manuel's father gave way to temptation and stole the money.

It was a crime that did him little good. For years his conscience troubled him and now, according to Manuel, the old man was dying. Wracked with guilt, he insisted that the £3,000 be returned to the clinic. At this point, Manuel looked Maria in the eye and told her he was counting on her to help him find the clinic. He even produced a bulging envelope which he said contained the cash.

Then the conversation took an even odder turn. Manuel suddenly said that they might be helped by a man who was now coming along the street towards them. Maria followed his gaze. The man approaching was about 36 years old, handsome, with long hair, penetrating eyes and a flowing moustache. His name, although she didn't know it at the time, was Antonio Manuel Matos Amaro. Antonio stopped and offered to help. He spoke Portuguese, told Maria he came from Brazil and asked her if she was having a good time over here in England. Then he shook her hand.

At once Maria went cold. She felt strange, as if he'd somehow given her a drug. Antonio looked at her intently and she lost awareness of what was happening. Then she heard him tell her firmly, "Go and draw out all your savings, get all your jewellery and don't tell anyone. Then come back here and we'll be waiting for you."

Astonishingly, Maria neither questioned this ridiculous order nor refused to obey it. Instead she caught a bus home, found her savings book and went to her building society where she drew out £900, every penny of savings she had. Then she went back home and collected not only her own jewellery, but that of her daughter as well. She was interrupted briefly by a phone call from her husband, but cut it short by hanging up on him.

With the cash and jewellery in her handbag, she used her own car to drive back to Notting Hill Gate. True to their word, Manuel and Antonio were waiting for her. The men seemed in high spirits. They asked if she had her money and jewellery in her handbag. When she confirmed that she had, Antonio said quickly, "Don't give it to me – we don't need it!" He then remarked that they didn't need money since they already had plenty and again showed her the fat envelope.

There was a branch of W. H. Smith nearby and Antonio went in to buy some paper he said he needed to prepare a document that clinic officials would have to sign swearing they'd got back their £3,000.

But when he came out of the newsagents, he was limping badly because a woman inside had run over his foot with a pram. He told Maria he was so severely injured he couldn't go to the Post Office to buy the stamp he needed to send the document back to Manuel's dying father in Portugal. He asked Maria if she'd go for him and offered to hold her handbag while she did so.

Maria handed him the bag and started to cross the road to the Post Office. Half way there she stopped suddenly. She couldn't remember where she was or how to get to the Post Office that was directly in front of her. She turned back. Manuel and Antonio had both disappeared. So had her handbag, her cash and her jewellery.

Maria went home and told her husband what had happened. He insisted she go to the police, but her story sounded so silly they had trouble taking it seriously. But it turned out Maria wasn't the only one who'd been robbed by the two men. Another victim later spotted Manuel on a bus and followed him home. Armed with an address, the police searched Manuel's flat and discovered large quantities of cash and jewellery.

During a ten-day trial at Southwark Magistrates Court, some astonishing stories emerged. One man had handed Manuel and Antonio £1,500, plus some Portuguese cash. Another gave them £6,000. A woman from Madeira was in the process of handing over £8,000 in cash when the police swooped and arrested the men. They were jailed for a year and a half, and then deported.

During the trial it emerged that Manuel's story about his father and the Dr John Smith Clinic was pure fiction. The envelope supposedly containing £3,000 was actually stuffed with cut newspaper backed by two £50 notes to make it look like a lot of cash. Antonio was not Brazilian as he claimed, but came from a town near Lisbon, in Portugal.

None of this is particularly surprising: the two men were clearly crooks prepared to say anything to persuade their victims to hand over large sums of money. But what remains absolutely astonishing is that their victims believed them.

Read Maria's story again and ask yourself if you – sweet, innocent and trusting though you may be – would have fallen for such an obvious cock-and-bull story? Maria herself told her husband she had no idea why she obeyed the orders given to her by the men. Their other victims were in the same boat. In case after case, something the Portuguese swindlers did turned their prey into temporary zombies. The question is ... what?

The theory has been put forward that the swindlers used drugs, but there was no evidence of this at their trial, none of their victims could remember being given a drug and no known drug produces precisely the effects Manuel and Antonio managed to achieve.

The science writer Robert Temple[11] interviewed Maria Milheiras at length and came to the conclusion that Antonio hypnotised her and the other victims. But he admitted the induction method was unknown. And there lies the problem.

[11] In his book *Open to Suggestion*, Temple opts for the idea that the swindlers simply kept trying their story on people until they found a few who were so suggestible they fell for it.

Maria and the others certainly seemed to be in some sort of trance that left them highly suggestible as many trance states do, but it wasn't a trance brought on by any known hypnotic technique.

The whole sorry episode might be written off as a fluke" if it wasn't for the fact that this sort of thing has happened before. In Heidelberg, Germany, in 1934, for example, a woman was arrested for the attempted murder of her husband. When she was examined by the police psychiatrist, he discovered that this was only one of six attempts and that the woman was acting on the orders of a criminal named Franz Walter.

The really interesting thing about the case was that Walter had met up casually with the woman on a train. She was off to consult a doctor about her stomach pains and when they got into conversation Walter told her he was a healer and homeopath. She was clearly intrigued by this because she agreed to go with him for a cup of coffee. But then he reached out to touch her hand and at once her will power deserted her. She went with him to his room where he placed her in trance simply by touching her forehead.

Thereafter the woman obeyed his every command, including working to earn him money, handing him 3,000 marks of her savings and, eventually, trying to murder her husband who, presumably, was getting in the way of a cosy arrangement. When the story came out, Walter was jailed for ten years.

An even earlier case involved a hairy beggar who knocked on a French cottage door in 1865. He pretended to be deaf and dumb and used pencil and paper to introduce himself as Timotheus Castellan, an unemployed cork-cutter who'd become a healer and dowser. The farm labourer who owned the cottage invited him in, gave him supper and let him sleep in a haystack.

Castellan repaid this kindness next day by raping the man's daughter. The girl, a 26-year-old named Josephine, was terrified of the repulsive Castellan, but he swamped her will by making strange signs in the air behind her back and later, as they were eating the mid-day meal, gesturing as if he was dropping something into her food.

This last action makes it sound as if a drug might have been involved, but in fact Josephine felt her senses leave her at once, before she ate anything more. Castellan carried her to the bedroom where she was completely unable to resist: when a neighbour came to knock at the door she wasn't even able to call out.

Afterwards, Castellan took her away with him. (Neighbours said she seemed upset and was making peculiar noises.) She stayed with him for three days, during which he repeatedly demonstrated his power over her. He could paralyse her with a sign, have her laugh hysterically to order and even crawl around on all fours like an animal. A local farmer, disgusted by these exhibitions, tried to send Castellan on his way, but as soon as they separated, Josephine became paralysed and Castellan had to be brought back to release her.

Josephine only broke free of his influence when he became distracted by a conversation with some hunters. While his attention was elsewhere, she ran away and returned home. It took her six weeks to recover from her ordeal, but Castellan was arrested and jailed for 12 years.

While criminals like Castellan and Walter were punished for their use of strange powers, others were rewarded – or at least got away with it. If you consult your history books for the time of the Russian Revolution, you'll find mention of a very strange character called Rasputin at the doomed Tsarist Court.

Grigory Rasputin was a peasant by birth, but had a religious turn of mind and became a *staretz*. The term is usually translated as 'wandering monk' but Rasputin was nothing like the monks you find in the monasteries of England today. He was a heavy drinker, a womaniser and had a lot of the shaman (person in touch with the spirit world) about him.

His reputation as a healer eventually reached the ears of the Russian Tsarina, who had very good reason to be interested. Her son, the young Tsarevich, heir to the Russian throne, had haemophilia, a hereditary condition in which the blood won't clot properly. This meant that the smallest cut – or even a bruise – could turn into a crisis.

The condition was well beyond the medical skills of the day (and isn't all that easy to treat even now) so that when the Tsarevich fell ill all the Court doctors could really do was stand around and hope. The Tsarina, who was both religious herself and superstitious, asked Rasputin to help. He laid hands on the child, who immediately began to recover.

Thereafter, Rasputin was called every time the Tsarevich got ill. Once the royal messengers found him in a gipsy camp too drunk to come to Moscow. Rasputin simply sent word that he would pray for the boy. He did and the Tsarevich again recovered.

As you might imagine, the healing talent earned Rasputin huge influence with the Tsarina and, through her, with the Tsar himself. But this wasn't his only strange power. Prince Yussupov, the man who eventually murdered Rasputin, told of their first meeting when the 'holy devil' caused him to fall into a paralysed state: "His power was immense. I felt it subduing me and diffusing warmth throughout the whole of my being. I lay motionless, unable to call out or stir."

An Armenian philosopher, G. I. Gurdjieff, who became extremely popular with some British academics during the 1930s, seemed to have much the same ability. The author Rom Landau said of their first meeting: "The feeling of physical weakness pervaded me more and more. I was sure that if I tried to get up, my legs would sag under me and I would fall to the floor."

Prince Yussupov (and many others) assumed Rasputin used hypnosis and the same was sometimes said of Gurdjieff, who had a dark, penetrating gaze. But here again, any known method of induction seems to be missing, so that some other factor must have come into play.

Gurdjieff, Rasputin and the criminals Castellan and Walter were all healers, which may give a clue to what that factor was. Many people believe that healing by the laying on of hands involves the transfer of a mysterious energy from the healer to the patient. It may be possible that this same energy can be directed to overcome people's will as well as heal them.

How far this can go is shown by the abilities of the British sorcerer and mystic Aleister Crowley, described by the popular press of his day as 'the wickedest man in the world'. Asked to demonstrate his powers on one occasion, he instantly persuaded a London bookseller that his shelves were empty, so that the man had to plead with him to bring back the books. On another, he caused a man to behave like a dog until he finally jumped through a window and disappeared for a whole day before returning with his clothes torn and face bleeding.

Crowley's own explanation of his powers was simple and didn't involve either healing energy or hypnosis. He said he used magic.

Chapter 11

Magic of the mind

A leister Crowley learned his 'magic' in a secret brotherhood called the Hermetic Students of the Golden Dawn. It had many respectable members, including the the Irish poet W. B. Yeats, who was head of the organisation for a while. The lifetime of the Golden Dawn was relatively short. It was founded in 1888 and started to fall apart in 1900. But members got up to many strange things while it lasted.

Entry into the organisation was by invitation and initiation, much like the Freemasons, but a lot more creepy. Describing one initiation, *Times* contributor Sean Thomas wrote:

> *The temple walls were richly adorned with kabbalah symbols and Egyptian hieroglyphs. In the middle was*

an empty coffin, a cuboid altar and a table decked with chalice, knife and scourge (whip). In the smoky shadows, red-robed priests and priestesses patrolled about the room, chanting the Dawn's weird prayers as they went.'

Aleister Crowley

What happened once you were in? Crowley himself complained sourly that, during his initiation, the Golden Dawn, "bound me with fearsome oaths, then revealed to me the Signs of the Zodiac and the letters of the Hebrew alphabet."

There was some truth to this claim. The 'First Knowledge Lecture' to Golden Dawn students did indeed deal with the Signs of the Zodiac and the letters of the Hebrew alphabet, but it also introduced mind-training. They involved breath control, visualisation, meditation, contemplation and various other mental gymnastics.

In other words, behind the smoky shadows and the chanting, red-robed priests, the Golden Dawn was quietly teaching its members a form of mind-training that was similar in some respects to Eastern yoga, but concentrated very strongly on the art of visualisation.

Even the rituals of the Order involved visualisation, known to initiates as their 'inner aspect'. It wasn't enough to dress up in robes and parade about waving wands and chanting. You had at the same time to visualise exactly and in detail all sorts of things that were going on invisibly. In one rite, for example, you were supposed to imagine blue fire ('like the flame from burning methylated spirits') emerging from the tips of your fingers as you drew a geometrical shape in the air.

At more advanced levels, visualisation training became so intense that the initiate learned to imagine things so vividly they appeared to be physically present. This reached the point of becoming a controlled hallucination, involving not just sight, but all the senses. When asked to visualise a rose, it wasn't enough just to see it as if you were really holding the flower in your hand – you had to be able to smell its scent, feel its texture and even taste the dew on its petals. If you visualised a bell, you had to be able to hear the sound when you rang it. And so on.

This was mind-training of a very high order and suggests that the 'magical' effects created by Golden Dawn members – like Crowley's curious ability to control others – actually came about through the exercise of some sort of mental power. In fact, one Golden Dawn initiate went so far as to define magic as, 'the art and science of changing consciousness at will'.

But what made it really weird was the results the Golden Dawn achieved from this form of mind-training, results that went far beyond anything Crowley ever demonstrated in public. The organisation itself was structured in a series of levels or grades. You moved from one grade to another by attending meetings and doing the work, but some required a special examination which involved not only written papers, but practical demonstrations.

At one level, you were required to conjure up a spirit so that it became visible to your examiner, 'at least to the consistency of incense smoke'. Was such a thing really possible?

Chapter 12
Creatures of the mind

The scene was a small camp in the mountains of Tibet. It was brutally cold and the air was thin. The ground was rocky and barren, but at least it lay below the snow line. The travellers were a mixed bunch, all but one of them Tibetan, all but one of them male. The exception, their leader, was literally unique. She was the only European woman Lama in the whole of Tibet. And she had just seen something that made her doubt her own eyes.

Alexandra David-Neel began to travel at an early age, partly inspired by the science fiction of her fellow-countryman, Jules Verne. Soon she had explored most of Europe, then returned briefly to her native France before setting her sights on somewhere more exotic. She travelled to India, then used her political connections – and her husband's money – to do something no other European woman had ever managed to do before: she crossed the border into Tibet … and stayed, with one short break, for more than 20 years.

During this time she witnessed many strange sights, but none anything like what she was seeing now. Moments before, a lone traveller had stumbled into her camp, wild-eyed, distracted, possibly a little feverish. She recognised him at once as a well-known Tibetan artist she'd met years before, although he'd changed greatly in the interim. Then he had been relaxed. Now he seemed nervous and ill-at-ease.

But none of this was what caught Madame David-Neel's attention. Her eyes were riveted on

the monstrously large, shadowy presence that hovered just beyond his left shoulder, its shape no more solid than the last wisp of morning mist, yet distinctly, visibly *there*.

For many years now, Madame David-Neel had studied the complex religion of Tibet, poring over its ancient texts and examining its art. She recognised the looming figure at once. It was one of the many fearsome gods believed to inhabit the Land of Snows.

Was she really in the presence of some god or demon? Madame David-Neel couldn't quite believe it. With one wary eye on the ghostly figure, she began to question the traveller it haunted. What emerged was intriguing.

Like most Tibetan artists, the man had always selected religious themes for his paintings. But since their last meeting, he had formed a special devotion to a particular deity. He meditated on it daily and, using old scriptures for reference, painted its image again and again. He showed Madame David-Neel one of those paintings now. The image was of the figure that lurked semi-visibly behind him.

Although Madame David-Neel was a Buddhist by this stage of her life, she could not quite bring herself to accept that a Tibetan god had answered this man's prayers and now followed him around like a pet dog. Instead, what sprang to her mind was a very curious Tibetan doctrine she'd heard a long time ago: the doctrine of the *tulpa*.

Tulpas, according to the ancient monastic lore looked and behaved much like spirits, but were not real ghosts. Rather they were creations of the human mind, similar to the fictional characters dreamed up by an author, but having taken on a life of their own and somehow become visible not just to their creator, but to others as well. They were, in short, thought-forms made real.

Madame David-Neel was not sure she'd

believed this peculiar doctrine, but now she'd seen a *tulpa* for herself, she decided to experiment. After the artist and his weird companion went on their way, she began a daily regime of meditation during which she strongly visualised a plump and cheerful little monk, rather like Friar Tuck in the story of Robin Hood.

At first she bent her efforts on seeing the monk as vividly as possible in her mind's eye. She paid careful attention to detail, right down to the colour of his eyes, the cut of his robe, the shape of his feet. All this, of course, was just a vivid mental picture, the sort of thing you might conjure up if you were day-dreaming.

But once she had all the details in place, she switched to visualising the monk as if he was actually standing in front of her. This was difficult at first but got easier with practice and after several weeks she was finally able to see the little monk as if he were really there[13].

This was, of course, quite different to what happened to the Tibetan artist who believed he was meditating on a real god, but all the same, strange things started to happen. One day she

[13] You'll notice that what Madame David-Neel was doing was very similar to the Golden Dawn visualisation training with the rose.

spotted her little monk walking through the camp *even though she hadn't visualised him.* He disappeared behind a tent and when she followed he was no longer there. But a day or two later, he was back again, still without any visualisation on her part.

Thereafter, the appearances became more and more frequent. More alarmingly, Madame David-Neel noticed the monk himself was beginning to change. He lost weight and took on a thin, sinister appearance. The crisis point arrived when another member of her party asked her who the new arrival was. She realised her tulpa had slipped out of her control.

From her studies, Madame David-Neel knew that since the creature was essentially a projection from her own mind, there was no way of destroying it. The only thing she could do was reabsorb it. Which is what she did do, but only after weeks of effort: the *tulpa* fought for independent life as fiercely as a trapped animal.

The David-Neel report is not the only example of Tibetan thought-form projection. Certain mystics in that strange land are reputed to have used it as a bizarre 'teaching aid' to get across a difficult, but basic, Buddhist doctrine. Typically what might happen was this:

A spiritual teacher (guru) would tell a favoured pupil (chela) that he had progressed so far there was nothing more he could learn from a fellow human and he now needed to make contact with a special teaching deity, known as a *yidam*, who could take him further. The only other thing the guru could do was explain how a *yidam* might be called up.

The method of contact was actually quite creepy. The pupil was sent off to find a remote, isolated cave high up in the Himalayas. There he was instructed to draw a magic circle called a *kylkhor*. This was a complicated business using coloured sands that could take several weeks to complete.

Then, after studying religious images and texts about the *yidam*, the pupil was instructed to visualise the creature as appearing inside the *kylkhor*. Like the Golden Dawn members, he was told to make the visualisation as detailed and realistic as possible and to continue with the operation until the creature seemed to be physically present.

Kylkhor

When the pupil reported back that he had evoked the *yidam* to visible appearance, the guru would tell him this was not enough: he needed to be able to hear the deity's words. So the pupil went back to the cave and worked on imagining conversations with the *yidam* until it seemed he could actually hear the creature talking to him.

Although the god could now take over teaching the pupil, the old guru would suggest the pupil needed to receive the *yidam*'s blessing. In Tibet, a blessing is imparted by laying hands on somebody's head, so this instruction meant that the chela had to imagine the *yidam* so vividly he could actually feel it.

Finally, the pupil was asked to continue his meditations and visualisations until the *yidam* was able to leave the *kylkhor*. At this point the entire exercise was complete. The pupil had successfully called up a god who would accompany him for the rest of his life, guiding him in everything he did. The problem was, some pupils didn't buy it.

One or two rebellious students would go back to their gurus and explain that they had doubts about the creature in the kylkhor. Specifically, they wondered if it really was a god or just something they made up with all their concentration and visualisation. Typically, their guru would point out their *yidam* was now as solid as the Himalayas and send them back to the cave with instructions to meditate until they weeded out all doubts.

But if that didn't work, the guru would eventually congratulate the student on achieving an important realisation. The *yidam* was indeed the product of the student's mind ... just like everything else in the physical world. For

Buddhists believe the entire universe is *maya*, an illusion generated by the human mind.

From the Tibetan experience, it seems possible that the intensive mental training undergone by members of the Golden Dawn did not, as they believed, enable them to call up spirits, but rather to create living thought-forms that could, on occasion, become visible to others. And that wasn't the only strange power the training produced.

Chapter 13

'Skrying in the spirit vision'

Many members of the Golden Dawn firmly believed that aspects of its training helped them develop what they called 'spirit vision' – a mysterious ability to 'see' things in their mind's eye that were actually happening far away.

This is a strange power that seems to have been around for a very long time. Shamans in Tibet, Siberia, Africa, India and the Americas all have a reputation for using it that dates back to prehistory. The first scientific experiment designed to prove it really happens was carried out, astoundingly, back in 550 BC.

According to the historian Heroditus, Croesus, the wealthy King of Lydia, was interested in obtaining some political advice from an oracle (priest or priestess through whom a god speaks);

and the most famous oracles at the time were all in Greece. In an age when everybody believed in oracles, the problem was deciding which was best. What Croesus did was send messengers to seven Greek oracles challenging each of them to say what he (Croesus) was doing at a specific time on a particular day.

When the day and time arrived, he decided to make it really difficult. Instead of following his usual routine (which an oracle might have hit on by guesswork) he did something no king ever did in those days – he set out to prepare a meal for himself. Since he wasn't up to anything elaborate, he put together a stew. But to make sure this was *really* beyond guesswork, he selected a mixture of lamb and tortoise for his ingredients.

When the messengers reported back, six of the oracles were complete failures. But the seventh – the world famous Oracle of Delphi – got every element of the test correct ... even down to the fact that the cauldron Croesus used had a peculiar brass lid. The Priestess at Delphi had used the Golden Dawn's 'skrying in the spirit vision' – now called 'remote viewing' – to see exactly what he was up to.

Oracle at Delphi

Professionals like shamans and oracles weren't the only ones to exhibit the strange power of remote viewing. Emanuel Swedenborg, a respected Swedish scholar and scientist of the 18th century, seems to have developed It quite spontaneously.

Swedenborg was born the son of a bishop and educated at the University of Uppsala where he showed himself to be an outstanding scholar with a particular talent for languages, mathematics and the sciences. After he qualified, the Swedish King appointed him special assessor to the Royal College of Mines. Thereafter he pursued a scholarly career, publishing scientific papers and inventing things like air guns, until at the age of 56, something extraordinary happened.

Swedenborg went to bed one night and dreamed a vivid dream in which he was transported to the spirit worlds. It was the start of something life-changing. From that point on, the quiet scholar began to have an almost endless stream of visions, dreams, trances and illuminations during which he was a frequent visitor to both Heaven and Hell, spoke with God and communicated with angels and the spirits of the dead.

On one occasion he was shown the order of the universe. To his surprise – and perhaps dismay – it was quite different from the picture portrayed by the Christian Church, which he had believed in all his life. He decided he had been appointed by God as a spiritual messenger whose job was to visit the higher planes of existence and report back to the rest of humanity on what he found there.

Swedenborg took this divine appointment so seriously that he packed in his government job and retired on half-pay in order to devote himself to his spiritual studies. He stopped eating meat and went on a diet composed mainly of bread, milk and coffee. When he began to report conversations with Plato, Aristotle and other long-dead philosophers, many of his friends decided he'd gone mad.

Although there is now a minority religion based on his teachings, it would be tempting to imagine his friends might have been right were it not for the fact that Swedenborg, like the Oracle of Delphi, exhibited strange powers, among them remote viewing.

In 1759, for example, he was attending a dinner party in Gothenburg. For the first couple of hours, the occasion went off pleasantly, then Swedenborg began to feel peculiar, excused himself and left the room. He returned some time later in an agitated state to announce that a fire had broken out in the Swedish capital Stockholm and was spreading rapidly. Throughout the remainder of the evening, Swedenborg kept disappearing from the room, then returning with news of the fire's progress. He was hugely relieved when the blaze was finally put out just three houses away from his own home.

Today, this sort of incident would hardly be remarkable. You'd assume the person concerned was listening to a radio, watching news reports on television, or just talking to Stockholm friends on his mobile phone. But in the 18th century, the fastest form of transport was a galloping horse and news spread very slowly.

The following day, the Governor of Gothenburg got to hear of Swedenborg's strange behaviour and summoned him to give an account of his weird vision. Swedenborg obliged with a highly detailed account of how the Stockholm fire had started, how it had spread and how it had finally been put out. Two days later, a courier arrived from the capital with a report that confirmed every word Swedenborg had said.

By the time Swedenborg died in 1772, Franz Mesmer had made a name for himself throughout Europe and, by the turn of the century, both mesmerists and early hypnotists were growing very excited by the fact that some of their subjects managed to give detailed descriptions of distant events and locations. A few even managed the repulsive feat of seeing into people's stomachs and reporting on what they'd just eaten.

Since science no longer believes in what was then called 'travelling clairvoyance' the work done by these early pioneers is now largely ignored. But experimentation continued throughout the 20th century and into the 21st century.

In 1972, scientists Russel Targ and Hal Puthoff established a research project at the Stanford

Research Institute in California and concluded after ten years work involving several hundred experimental trials that remote viewing is a talent some people exhibit quite naturally. More interesting still, they discovered that many people could be trained in the art.

Several of the results they achieved were spectacular. One star subject, Ingo Swann, managed to guide a submarine to the wreck of a sunken ship using nothing more than his remote viewing ability. Other subjects were taught to see into sealed boxes and even read data from microdots – something impossible with the naked eye.

ARV: the Key to Fame and Fortune

ARV – Associative Remote Viewing – was a variation on the basic talent that developed out of the Stanford research. It involved attempts to remote view into the future.

In one set of experiments, a group of investors played the Stock Market in accordance with ARV results obtained by a test subject named Keith Harary ... and made a staggering $100,000 profit.

But for reasons they cannot yet explain, the excited scientists were unable to repeat this highly successful experiment.

In the early 21st century, I played a small part in a successful remote viewing experiment set up by an engineering professor named Arthur J. Ellison, who was at the time Vice President of the Society for Psychical Research. Arthur was kind enough to contact me to say that he had enjoyed some of my books and mentioned his proposed experiment in the course of our correspondence. The result was that my wife, the artist, author and therapist Jacquie Burgess, volunteered to become one of his test subjects.

Arthur set up the test by placing a random 3-digit number on top of the bookcase in his study. He reported what happened next in his book *Science and the Paranormal*:

"I had no idea how my new ... volunteer from Ireland would find her way to my house ... so I thought that directions might be a good idea. I made a map from a well-known part of London to my house... (but) she needed none of this... Her husband wrote to me after the first 'visit' ... (with) the 3-digit number ... and – to my delight – two of the digits were correct. I changed the digits for three more... We did the experiment again three more times and, to my growing delight, each time she got two of the three digits correctly ... The chances of getting two out of three four times in a row was ... one chance in about 2,000."

The result didn't surprise me. Years before I'd tried a remote viewing experiment of my own with a volunteer hypnotic subject named Denise, who was required to examine a note left for her more than 160 kilometres away (100 miles away). She wasn't able to read the note[14], but she did manage

14 She said it was 'too dark to see'.

to determine, quite correctly, whether it was typed, handwritten or in block capitals, the colour of the paper, whether it was blank or ruled and how many lines were in the message. She was even able to count the number of words.

But this experiment went beyond simple remote viewing into the overlapping area of another strange power, which scientists now call OOBE or Out-of-Body Experience.

Chapter 14

Giving up the ghost

One of the first short stories I ever got published was a little bit of nonsense called *House Haunting*. It was about a young couple looking for a new home.[15] After several disappointments, they happened on their dream house, a property that suited both of them exactly... *and* one with a *For Sale* sign. They called the estate agent to make inquiries. He said he would meet them at the house and give them all the details there.

But when they met, what he told them sounded too good to be true. The house was in excellent repair, but the asking price was ridiculously low and it had been on the market for a suspiciously long time. They asked him to come clean and tell them what was wrong. The estate agent hesitated for a

[15] That's to say they were house hunting, thus allowing the title of my story to make a pleasing pun, which I'm sure you have already noticed.

while before admitting that the house was haunted. Then he added, in the proud punchline of my story, "But don't worry, Madam – you're the ghost!"

As a short story it wasn't up to much (as you've probably already realised) but it did have one interesting aspect: it was based on a real-life case history. The people concerned – a family by the name of Butler – lived in Ireland and were rather older than my fictional couple. For several years before the estate-agent incident, the wife had daydreamed obsessively about the sort of home she wanted, imagining herself walking through its corridors and rooms.

One day, while driving in the country with her husband, she suddenly spotted exactly the house she had imagined. It had no For Sale sign, but they contacted a local estate agent who knew the owner and a viewing was arranged. Before they entered the house, the wife told the estate agent she was going to describe the interior and did so in considerable detail. She was only wrong about one thing: a green door that didn't exist. But the agent was able to confirm such a door had existed at one time. It had been bricked up some time earlier.

Many years later, while attending a conference on the edge of Dartmoor, a schoolteacher told me an eerily similar story. She'd spent an afternoon daydreaming about a school trip she'd been unable to attend. The following school day one of her colleagues told her he'd not only seen her on the trip, but actually talked to her[16]. This sort of thing happens to schoolteachers. There was one in Europe who lost 18 jobs because her pupils kept seeing two of her – the real one and a phantom. Sometimes they stood side by side, sometimes the phantom walked the grounds while the physical teacher was inside[17].

What's happening here? The answer is a strange one. It seems that some people, under some circumstances, can leave their physical bodies and wander about the world like a ghost ... without the inconvenience of having to die to do it. In fact it seems that quite a lot of people can leave their bodies in this way. Research shows that about a quarter of all British students – and more than a third of the really clever ones – have had the experience at some time, often around the age of

16 You'll find fuller details of this strange story in my *The Ghosthunter's Handbook* published by Faber, London, 2004.

17 You'll find a little bit more about this in *The Ghosthunter's Handbook* as well.

puberty. For a few of them it spells trouble. I once met a girl who was diagnosed epileptic and placed on heavy medication after reporting an Out-of-Body Experience to her doctor.

How to Leave Your Body

(Golden Dawn Style)

Although many Out-of-Body Experiences occur spontaneously, members of the Golden Dawn believed you could learn, with training, how to leave your body at will. The method they used was a closely guarded secret. Until now...

Start by relaxing your body completely. Imagine a life-size figure standing in front of you a few feet away.

Visualise this figure walking around the room.

When you are comfortable with this visualisation, try to imagine what the figure is seeing as it walks around the room. Make notes and compare the results with what is really there.

Once you have successfully imagined the figure inspecting everything actually present in the room, transfer your consciousness to the figure through a fresh act of imagination and try to see the room through its eyes as it makes the next circuit.

Repeat this exercise until you experience a mental 'click-over' and find yourself out of your physical body, functioning in the body you have been imagining.

Scientific investigation of OOBEs only really began in the mid 1920s when a psychical researcher named Hereward Carrington decided to look into them. At first, the only hard information he could find was a series of experiments carried out in France, the results of which he described as 'most inadequate.' But then he received a letter from a 25-year-old American, Sylvan Muldoon.

Muldoon, a sickly individual, not only maintained he was able to leave his physical body at will, but claimed he'd been doing so since the age of 12. He later described the experience in these words:

"I dozed off to sleep about ten thirty o'clock ... and slept for several hours. At length I realized I was slowly awakening, yet I could not seem to drift back into slumber nor further arouse....

"Gradually ... I became more conscious of the fact that I was lying somewhere ... and shortly I seemed to know that I was reclining upon a bed ... I tried to move ... only to find that I was powerless — as if adhered (stuck) to that on which I rested... one feels fairly glued down, stuck fast, in an immovable position.

"Eventually the feeling of adhesion relaxed, but was replaced by another sensation equally unpleasant — that of of floating;... My entire rigid body — I thought it was my physical, but it was my astral body — commenced vibrating at a great rate of speed in an up-and-down direction and I could feel a tremendous pressure being exerted in the back of my head ... This pressure was very impressive and came in regular spurts, the force of which seemed to pulsate my entire body...

"When able to see, I was more than astonished! No words could possibly explain my wonderment. I was floating! I was floating in the very air, rigidly horizontal, a few feet above the bed... Slowly, still zigzagging with the strong pressure in the back of my head, I was moved towards the ceiling, all the while horizontal and powerless ...

"Involuntarily, at about six feet (1 metre) above the bed, as if the movement had been conducted by an invisible force present in the very air, I was uprighted from the horizontal position to the perpendicular and placed standing upon the floor of the room. There I stood for what seemed to me about two minutes, still powerless to move of my own accord, and staring straight ahead ...

"Then the controlling force relaxed. I felt free, noticing only the tension in the back of my head. I took a step, when the pressure increased for an interval and threw my body out at an acute angle. I managed to turn round.

"There were two of me! I was beginning to believe myself insane. There was another 'me' lying quietly upon the bed! It was difficult to convince myself that this was real, but consciousness would not allow me to doubt what I saw."[18]

18 Quoted from *The Projection of the Astral Body* by Sylvan Muldoon and Hereward Carrington.

Dr. Carrington was impressed. He visited Muldoon and conducted experiments to test his claims. These were so successful, Carrington promptly put his reputation on the line by co-authoring a book about Muldoon's experiences. Although sceptics continue to insist the sensation of leaving your body is a hallucination, controlled experiments have shown there's more to it than that. For example, the American psychologist Charles Tart set up something similar to the remote viewing test devised for my wife by Professor Ellison.

Tart left a target five-digit number on a shelf 1 ½ metres above the bed of his subject in such a position that it could only be read by looking down from above. For four nights the subject went to sleep normally and nothing of interest happened. On the fifth, she reported an OOBE during which she floated up to the ceiling and was able to look down on the hidden number. Tart asked her what the number was and she replied correctly that it was 25132. The odds against this being guesswork have been calculated at 99,999 to one.

Another subject who undertook an Out-of-Body Experience was unable to read the target number, but did manage to spot two lab assistants who had wandered into the room at the time. Perhaps the most interesting results of all were obtained by the Latvian scientist Karlis Osis who experimented with a subject named Alex Tanous. In a rather complicated set-up, Tanous was required to leave his body to look at some target pictures. But the pictures were placed in such a way that they could only be viewed from a specially constructed chamber. This chamber was not only shielded but fitted with highly sensitive sensor plates and strain gauges. When Tanous reported (correctly) on the pictures he was viewing while out of the body, the gauges in the shielded chamber became active.

While this suggests you really do have some sort of ghostly 'second body' inside you – and one that can actually be weighed using sensitive enough equipment – more research clearly needs to be done. This is especially true in the light of an experiment carried out by Hereward Carrington in which he became his own subject of investigation.

For the experiment, Carrington several times willed himself to project his body into the presence of a woman who had a reputation as a psychic. Absolutely nothing happened and he judged the test a failure ... until the woman in question reported waking to find him standing in her room at the exact times he was trying for his OOBEs. She said he remained for a few moments before fading away.

Chapter 15

Fear of floating

While many of those describing OOBEs have reported floating up near the ceiling, there seem to have been a fearless few who managed the same feat without leaving their bodies. The process is known as levitation.

Levitation isn't quite the same as flying. The word comes from the Latin *levis* meaning 'light' (in the sense of having little weight) which gives the clue to what it's all about. When something levitates, it's as if it grows so light that it floats up in the air without any visible cause or means of support. In short, it just defies the law of gravity.

Clearly levitation – of people or objects – doesn't happen every day, but reports of the phenomenon go back a very long time. During the time of Christ, for example, a sorcerer named

Simon Magus is said to have challenged St Peter to a sort of magical duel at the Roman Forum. It looked as if St Peter had lost when Simon suddenly floated high above the ground. But Peter fell to his knees and prayed that God would halt the deception. Simon promptly plunged to his death.

Despite this people were at it again just a few hundred years later. In the 4th century AD, the magician Chrysanthius and the philosopher Iamblichus both experienced levitation. In Tibet, the great Buddhist yogi (holy man), Milarepa, was said to be able to walk, sit and even sleep while levitating.

In the East, the power of levitation was seen in Brahmins (priests) and fakirs (magicians) in India and the Ninja warriors of Japan. This was accomplished through secret breathing and visualisation exercises that influenced a universal energy variously known as *prana*, *ch'i* or *ki*. In the West, this ability is more often associated with the intervention of God and levitators are seen as saints – or at least as saintly people. In the 17th century, St Joseph of Cupertino often gave a little shriek and levitated according to eyewitness accounts. St Teresa of Avila also suffered from 'a great force beneath her feet' that lifted her up at the most inconvenient times. She hated the experience and frequently asked God to stop making a show of her. In more recent times, a Carmelite nun was reported to have floated to the top of a tree, while another flew gracefully up a flight of stairs.

Not all these reports are necessarily genuine. The Japanese Ninjas trained in spectacular jumps as part of their martial art and may have given the impression of levitation when they were doing nothing of the sort. The great Russian ballet dancer, Nijinsky, became world famous for a leap during which he seemed to pause for a moment in mid air, but this was an optical illusion rather than levitation.

Even the Indian fakirs are sometimes capable of faking it. A 19th century French judge named Louis Jacolliot reported how one 'uttered appropriate incantations' before rising gradually over half a metre from the ground and remaining there, floating like a Buddha. For 20 minutes, Jacolliot tried to figure how the man could 'fly in the face... of all known laws of gravity' but the fakir did not float entirely unaided – he was supported by a cane held in his right hand. The stunt still looked spectacular – it was certainly enough to impress the judge – but has been repeated many times in the West by stage conjurers.

How to Levitate Your Friends

There's an experiment in levitation – or something very close to it – you can try out with the help of a group of your friends.

Have one (brave) person sit in the middle of the room in a straight-backed chair without arms – an ordinary kitchen chair is ideal. The person selected should be at least of average height and build, but results will be more spectacular if he or she is large. Make sure you are not experimenting in a low-ceilinged room and that there are no light fittings or ceiling ornaments immediately above them.

Pick two people of roughly equal size and height and have them stand one on either side of the person on the chair. Invite them to place the first two fingers of each hand behind the victim's knee and underneath his arm.

Now ask them to lift him carefully out of the chair, using just their fingers. In all probability they will find this extremely difficult, if not completely impossible.

At this point the experiment proper can begin. With the two 'lifters' in position at the sides (but *without* yet touching the subject) have all those participating gather around the person in the chair and place their hands on the top of his head. (The hands should be placed interlaced. That's to say you might begin by placing your right hand on the subject's head. This would be followed by the right hand of the person next to you, then your left hand, then the next person's left hand, then the following person's right hand and so on, making a tower of interlaced hands. Both lifters should have their hands interlaced in the tower as well.)

Tell the subject to relax as much as possible, then, as a group, begin to apply pressure downwards on his head. You need to press down firmly – but not so firmly as to break his neck – for about half a minute. During that period, the group should chant the word 'Light... light... light...' in unison, gradually getting louder and louder.

If you do this properly you'll quickly become aware of a sort of rising excitement as the energy of the group increases. At the point when this excitement peaks (which you'll learn to judge from experience, although 30 seconds chanting will usually do it) you should call out loudly, "NOW!"

On this signal, everyone should immediately stop chanting and the two lifters should place their fingers back in position behind the knees and under the armpits as quickly as possible then lift upwards. Carried out properly, the placing of the fingers and the lift should take place in a single, fluid motion.

If the experiment goes well, the person in the chair will shoot upwards well above head height for a tiny fraction of the effort needed to lift him before.

> When this happens, the group as a whole should be prepared to catch him to make sure he doesn't hurt himself on the way down.

All the same, there's a lot of evidence that genuine levitation really happens. One well-proven – and very creepy – case occurred in 1906 when a 16-year-old South African schoolgirl, Clara Germana Cele began to show what were taken to be symptoms of demonic possession. During one of her seizures, she suddenly levitated over 1 ½ metres off the bed.

It proved to be the first of many such incidents and she later showed she could levitate in an upright position as well as horizontally. Priests called in to deal with the possession quickly discovered that if she was sprinkled with holy water she would come crashing down again, but the treatment unfortunately did not stop the levitation happening.

Somebody who could do it without the aid of demons was the Scots medium Daniel Dunglas Home, an extraordinary figure who astonished Victorian society with his strange powers. Home's mother was psychic and his own abilities appeared at a very early age – when he was only four he correctly predicted the death of a cousin.

The Spiritualist craze was in full swing during his lifetime and he attended many seances (where spirits of the dead are contacted). But oddly enough he thought most mediums were frauds and avoided any close contact with them. When he started to hold his own seances, however, all sorts of strange things happened – ghostly lights shone our of nowhere, raps were heard, phantom hands reached out of the air to shake hands with sitters, spectral instruments played music, tables tipped and spirits communicated. This was usual for Spiritualism, but where Home's seances differed from those of almost every other medium in the country was that they took place with the lights on.

Home proved to have abilities no other medium could match, including a weird control over his physical body that allowed him to grow or shrink at will. On one occasion he increased his height to over 2 metres, 28 centimetres taller than usual. On another he shrank 18 centimetres to a height of 1½ metres. He experienced his first levitation at the age of 19 while visiting the home of a Connecticut silk manufacturer. Both he and his host were astonished when the young man abruptly floated off the ground.

Home had no control over the ability at first, but eventually became able to levitate at will. Eyewitnesses claimed that once off the ground he was actually able to fly as well as float. In 1868, he demonstrated the ability in a spectacular  manner before the guests at a dinner party in the home of Lord Adare. As the party watched in astonishment, Home went into trance, levitated then floated out through one third-storey window and back in through another before settling gently to the ground.

Home not only levitated himself, but demonstrated the strange power of levitating various objects – an ability he shared with a great many other mediums. One of the objects most favoured for influencing in this way was the heavy Victorian-style table.

Chapter 16

Table-turning

It happened at a conference centre nestling in the shadow of the Malvern Hills in England. Almost 40 people, broken into groups of four or five, were seated around different tables placed randomly across a large room. It might have been the seating plan for a busy restaurant lunch, but there were no plates on the tables.

More to the point, it was long past midnight, every window was blacked out with heavy blinds and the room was lighted only by a scattering of night-lights, leaving it in almost total darkness. The occasion was to attempt an experiment of a very odd kind – the art of table-turning.

Table-turning became immensely popular as part of the Spiritualist movement that swept across America and Europe during the Victorian era, where mediums attempted to contact the dead. Groups would meet regularly in darkened rooms, seated round the heavy polished tables that were fashionable at the time. The hands of each sitter would be placed on the surface of the table, sometimes in such a way that fingers touched, thus making a circle.

The session would often begin with a simple prayer, then a period of absolute silence before someone asked aloud, "Is anybody there?" By 'anybody' they meant any spirit, for the belief was that table-turning was somehow associated with spirit contact. If the group was lucky, the question would be answered by a mysterious knock. Then, given time, the table itself might begin to rock and tilt. Really fortunate groups might experience it lifting off the floor. This, then, was what was being attempted in the conference centre, although the organisers of the event had strong doubts about whether spirits would be involved.

The early part of the experiment did not prove promising. When the lights were lowered and the question asked, not a table trembled; and if there were any spirits present, they declined to knock. But later, on instructions, the groups round the various tables tried a different approach. And suddenly it happened.

"It's moving!" somebody exclaimed excitedly. "I distinctly felt it move!"

"You're imagining it," someone else said cynically.

But then the table jerked visibly with a movement that was clearly beyond the question of imagination. Within moments, it had started to rock violently. Then, as the sitters scattered their chairs in an effort to keep up, the table began to move jerkily across the floor, getting faster and faster as it went.

I was not quick enough to get out of the way. Seconds later, I was pinned against a wall – and stayed pinned until my colleagues pulled the table off me. The man who devised the system that produced this spectacular effect was a British psychologist named Kenneth Batcheldor. He was not a great believer in spirits, but he did take an interest in psychical research and had read numerous reports of table-turning in Victorian times. What intrigued him was that the phenomenon had quietly died out. For more than 50 years, there had been few – if any – reports of moving tables anywhere. Consequently, nobody could study the whole thing scientifically.

In the early 1960s, Batcheldor decided to do something about it. What he did was set up a group that would try to set tables moving again, exactly like the old Victorian Spiritualists. The approach was strictly scientific. There were no mediums involved and one of the group members was an engineer who was put in charge of setting up equipment that would record results in order to rule out human error. (The human mind being what it is, it's very easy to imagine you see – or even feel – small table movements when nothing is actually happening ... especially in a darkened room where everybody is over-excited about the possibility of spirit contact.)

For the first ten meetings, nothing happened – or at least nothing much. The table did move very slightly a few times, but no more than you'd expect from natural muscle twitches as the sitters' arms got tired. It was beginning to look as if proper table-turning had died with Queen Victoria.

Then, on the eleventh session, something crazy happened. To the astonishment and shock of everybody present, the table rose completely off the floor and floated in the air. Batcheldor stopped talking about muscle twitching. "It seemed," he reported later, "we had stumbled on a genuinely paranormal force."

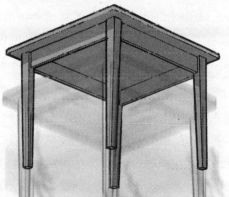

But what was the nature of the force? The Victorians had assumed it was spirit intervention. Batcheldor wasn't so sure and the group as a whole agreed to continue their experiments in the hope of finding the truth. The only way to do so, they believed, was to approach the whole thing with strict scientific controls.

The first levitation had taken place in total darkness, which meant the sitters only knew about it from the feel of the table and the sound it made falling back onto the floor. They were sure enough of what they'd experienced, but from a scientific point of view, they could have been mistaken. Batcheldor decided to tighten things up a bit.

To do this, he had a special device made. Pressure switches were attached to each foot of the table and attached to a small, battery-operated bulb set into the table-top. Each switch tripped in turn as the leg went clear of the floor, switched off again when the leg came down. The whole thing was so wired that the light only came on when all four legs were off the floor at once – in other words, only when the table was levitating.

This seemed fine and worked well enough, but Batcheldor wasn't entirely satisfied. First of all, the group discovered that the switches could trip when the table tilted to more than a 40 degree angle. After some discussion, they decided this didn't really make much difference since it was very easy to spot when the table was tilting. In other words, if the table tilted and the light came on, you had a false levitation. If there was no tilt when the light came on, then you could be sure the table was really off the ground.

But something else was worrying Batcheldor now. It occurred to him that when the group saw the bulb light up, they could be hallucinating. It would have to be a *collective* hallucination – something so rare that psychologists are split on whether it actually happens – but all the same he felt he shouldn't take any chances. So he replaced the bulb with a buzzer. Which doesn't sound much of a change, but made all the difference – a buzzer could be recorded in a darkened room, thus ruling out hallucination.

After a while he decided that wasn't good enough either and added more precautions in the form of photographs. He experimented with stereoscopic pictures (which have a 3D effect) and with different kinds of flash, including infra-red, which is invisible to the human eye.

Once he had the cameras in place, there were no more levitations for a time, although he did get a fascinating picture that showed the table tilting violently with a group member actually sitting on it. But what he did notice was that the cameras were creating unexpected problems. For one thing it was tricky to keep a camera trained on the table (which tended to skeeter off in all directions, rather like the table that pinned me to the wall at Malvern). For another, table phenomena lessened dramatically whenever a camera was present.

All the same, things did happen, if a lot less frequently. Batcheldor described what occurred in a typical two-hour sitting:

"There was always an initial period of waiting before anything happened... usually 5–10 minutes though it could be as short as one minute or as long as half an hour...

"The first signs of activity were usually creaks or cracking noises in the wood of the table... but these were interspersed with sharp taps, scrapings or soft thuds... In a few instances, the latter noises were unmistakably heard on our chairs, on the floor or on the walls.

"After a few minutes...the table usually performed two or three slides...along the floor for a few inches. After a further pause, the table would tilt up on two legs then drop again. Tilts and slides would then continue at intervals...

"As the sitting proceeded, the movements... usually increased in power and extent... Spontaneous phenomena which could occur in a sitting were: breezes, intense cold, lights, touchings, pulling back of sitters' chairs, movements of objects, 'gluing' of the table to the floor so that it could not be budged and 'apports'.[19]

But the most spectacular phenomenon was definitely levitation. This is how Batcheldor described the first time it happened after they had set up the pressure switches and the centre light:

"By its red glow we could clearly see our hands on top of the table. The table then seemed to act as an excited person would and proceeded to execute all

19 The term 'apport' is used by psychical researchers to describe the sudden appearance (usually dropped from somewhere near the ceiling) of small objects during seances.

> manner of very lively movements –
> rocking, swaying, jumping, dancing,
> tilting … it shook like a live thing even
> when totally levitated, almost shaking
> our hands off. Because the levitations
> were not very high, I said, 'Come on –
> higher!' At which the table rose up
> chest high and remained there for eight
> seconds."

At another sitting, the table lifted 5 inches (13 centimetres) off the floor, floated across the room then crashed into some other furniture against the wall … after which it rose up and crashed down with such force the sitters thought it would break. One of them counted a total of 84 levitations during the session.

Batcheldor and his group went on to complete a series of 200 experimental sittings. Of these 120 produced no results, but the remaining 80 were wild. By the time they were finished, the group had produced some 800 pages of written notes and 27 tape recordings.

By the 21st meeting, they'd reached the stage

where sitters could ask the table to do something and, most times, it would. As the experiments continued, there seemed to be an increase in some sort of energy at the sittings because the movements got stronger and more violent. In the end, three tables were smashed – one of which had a tubular metal frame.

What looked like spirit contact started to occur. Raps broke out and when a code was devised, the occasional message came through. There were ghostly breezes around the sitters' hands and, on occasion, moments of intense cold. Sitters felt something touch them, although nothing visible was present. A small stone was thrown across the room by invisible hands and a box of matches was sprinkled about.

But at the same time, Batcheldor noticed a curious pattern. Every time he introduced a new scientific control, the phenomena would die away, then, after a long period of time, begin to creep back in. If he introduced really tight controls all at once, the phenomena stopped completely. If he introduced them slowly and gradually, it continued.

Furthermore, none of the meetings involved prayer or a medium or any of the familiar Spiritualist routines. The sitters weren't even quiet or particularly serious – some of the best results came when they were chatting and telling jokes. Batcheldor began to suspect that spirits weren't involved at all. What he was dealing with was, up to now, an unsuspected power generated and directed by the group itself.

But if groups could smash tables with the power of their mind, why hadn't this been discovered before? And more to the point, why didn't it happen every time the group simply concentrated? Batcheldor started to form a theory. Suppose what blocked the mysterious power was belief? For most people, the idea that you can move a table just by thinking at it is absurd. What if it is this very belief that stops the table moving?

The more he thought about it, the more it made sense. In Victorian times, the Spiritualists firmly believed that spirits of the dead entered their seance rooms. This belief enabled the moving tables and other odd incidents since it never occurred to the sitters that they themselves were the cause: everything was left to the 'spirits' while the sitters' unconscious minds, freed from responsibility, got on with the job.

Although Batcheldor's own group had no such Spiritualist beliefs, he suspected much the same mechanism was at work. Sitting in the dark with your hands on a table is such an odd occupation that very few people know what to expect ... although they hope the table might move.

And move it certainly will. As arms get tired, involuntarily muscle jerks will make sure of it. A group with no experience may not be immediately aware of this and mistake these natural movements for something weird. This begins to break down the belief that table-turning is impossible. The collective mind of the group then begins to produce results that are *genuinely* paranormal.

At the same time, the rational part of the mind was lulled by the fact that (at the beginning) no firm controls were in place. The sittings took place in total darkness with no recording devices or cameras of any sort. If the table moved, it could be because somebody was cheating.

But as controls were introduced, you would expect the rational mind to get nervous and stop anything happening ... which was exactly what the group had experienced. Only when the rational mind got used to the new conditions would it relax enough to allow movements to start up again.

Out of all this, Batcheldor came up with a system. He suggested that if your group wanted to move a table, you started out with no scientific controls whatsoever and arranged sittings so that cheating would not only be possible, but actually easy. Then, when table movements started, either through natural causes or because somebody really was cheating, you very slowly, very gradually, very patiently began to introduce your controls. With each new control, you should expect everything to quiet down or stop, but if you were patient, movements would eventually start up again – this time under scientifically controlled conditions. If you kept going long enough, you should be able to produce absolute proof that a group could move a table – even levitate a table – using just the power of the mind.

And, while it never made the headlines, this is exactly what happened. Batcheldor published his ideas in 1966. Within a couple of years, independent groups were experimenting with his system. It worked like a charm. By 1979, no fewer than ten groups had succeeded in table-turning using the Batcheldor method, a clear indication that mindpower, not spirits, was at work.

But if a group mind could levitate a table, surely it should be possible for a single mind – perhaps even your mind – to do something similar?

Chapter 17

The power of mind

Back in 1934, Dr J. B. Rhine (the same Dr Rhine mentioned in chapter 8) met a heavy gambler. The man's favourite game was craps, which is particularly popular in America and played by rolling two matched dice in an attempt to score 7 or 11. (There's more to the game than that, but I don't want to be accused of encouraging gambling by going into details.) What intrigued Rhine was that the man claimed there were times when he got 'hot' and could mentally control the way the dice fell.

The idea that a certain mental state ('getting hot') can influence your luck is fairly common among serious gamblers. Rhine decided to test it. He set up a series of experiments – at first with his gambler friend, later with others – in which specially made dice were thrown by a mechanical arm.

The dice had to be specially made for a peculiar reason. The spots on an ordinary die are made by cutting out small hollows and the more spots you cut out, the lighter that face of the die becomes. This means that the face with six spots is the lightest of all and hence more likely to turn upwards. The effect is tiny and doesn't interfere with most dice games, but it would influence the results of Rhine's experiments, so he had perfectly balanced dice created. These dice had to be thrown mechanically to guard against the faint possibility that a really skilful player could somehow influence the roll by clever wrist action.

Despite these strict precautions, the results of his experiments showed some of his subjects really were able to influence the dice to a degree that lay well beyond chance. Rhine went on to discover that this ability, labelled psychokinesis or PK for short, was independent of both space and time. A subject didn't have to be close to the dice to get an effect and it was spookily possible to influence dice that were about to be rolled next just as easily as the dice that were being rolled now.

By the 1970s, a New York artist named Ingo Swann – somebody else we've already met in this book – showed under carefully controlled conditions that he could change the temperature of nearby objects just by concentrating on them and could also affect magnetic fields. Other subjects proved able to influence enzymes and bacteria. Some could stimulate plant growth. But a Russian woman named Ninel Kulagina showed the most spectacular powers.

The first anybody in the West heard about this remarkable woman was when the Soviet authorities denounced her as a fraud in *Pravda*, the official newspaper of the Communist Party. She was accused both of 'hobnobbing with unclean powers' and producing her results by means of magnets. The article went on to accuse her of swindling the public out of 5,000 roubles and selling imaginary refrigerators door to door.

But Soviet scientists took Kulagina very seriously indeed. Rumours began to circulate about a secret film that showed exactly what she was able to do … under conditions that completely ruled out hidden magnets or tricks.

For a time, the situation in Russia was like something out of a spy movie. Scientists were tailed and threatened with violence. There were phone calls in the dead of night and attempts to steal the movie. But the authorities couldn't keep the lid on it forever.

The movie was eventually screened – secretly – to Western journalists. This is what they saw – Ninel Kulagina, a woman in her forties, was seated at a large, round, white table in front of a lace-curtained window. She was wearing a short-sleeved blouse and plain skirt.

The movie itself was shot in her flat in what was then Leningrad and is now, since the collapse of the Soviet Union, St Petersburg. Everything that happened was witnessed by a five-man film crew, a team of scientists and several reporters. The experiment was under the direction of Dr Edward Naumov, a Russian biologist who had left his speciality to become one of the foremost investigators of the paranormal in the Soviet Union[20].

The flat had been thoroughly inspected to rule out any possibility of mechanical trickery. As the cameras began to roll, Dr Naumov laid out a variety of small objects on the table before Kulagina. First he set down what looked like a wristwatch, but proved on closer inspection to be a compass on a strap. Next, he carefully balanced a single cigarette upright on its end and laid out a small metal cylinder about the size of a salt-shaker, a pen top and a matchbox. Then he stepped back and the experiment began.

Kulagina reached out to hold her hands, palms downwards, about 15 centimetres above the compass, moving them gently in a tight, small

---

[20] This was the same Dr Naumov I mentioned briefly earlier in the book in connection with telepathic hypnosis.

circle. The camera tracked in on the compass, but nothing was happening. Kulagina concentrated in silence. Her pulse rate began to rise dramatically as her heart raced to a frightening 250 beats a minute. Still nothing else happened.

For fully 20 minutes, the scientific team could do nothing but wait and listen to the whir of the cameras. Then, without warning, the compass needle shivered. Kulagina's mysterious powers had begun to show themselves.

Within seconds, the needle was visibly moving. Slowly at first, but with gathering speed it began to spin. Then suddenly it wasn't just the needle that was moving, but the whole compass, strap and all. Impossibly, it spun round and round on the table.

Now she'd got into her stride, Naumov emptied the box of matches onto the table and moved the metal cylinder beside them.

He tossed the empty matchbox casually beside the cylinder. Her body shaking with strain, Kulagina moved her hands again. The wooden matches moved together to form a raft, then flowed to the edge of the table where they fell off, one by one. The metal cylinder moved to join them.

To show there were no hidden wires and air currents weren't involved, Naumov produced a large plexiglass tube. Inside it he put another batch of matches and a non-magnetic metal container. The tube made no difference. As Kulagina concentrated, the objects shuffled from side to side.

The movie took more than seven hours to complete. The cameras had to be shut down several times to allow Kulagina to rest. So great was the strain that she lost over 1 kilogram in weight during the first half hour and by the time the experiment was finished, she could neither speak nor see. For days afterwards, she suffered from pains in her arms and legs, bouts of dizziness and inability to sleep.

But the suffering was worth it. Now that the secret was out, other movies were made – more than ten in all – and scientists flocked to test this incredible woman. One described how the top of his fountain pen crawled across the table towards him, followed closely by a glass tumbler. Another told of an experiment during which she separated an egg yolk from the white from a distance of 2 metres, then put them back together again.

A Russian writer, Vadim Marin, witnessed Kulagina 'call' a piece of bread towards her while eating a meal. The slice jerked across the table and jumped into her mouth. A journalist watched with horror during an interview as his lunchtime sandwich crawled away from his hand while Kulagina grinned mischievously.

But you don't have to go to Russia to witness personal PK in action. A few years ago while I was having supper with friends, my host suggested we slip away from the dining room as he wanted to show me something. He brought me up to a bedroom on the first floor where there was a mobile hanging from the ceiling above the bed. "Watch this," he said; and pointed.

After a moment, the mobile began to spin. I closed the door behind me and glanced around to make sure no open window was causing a draft. But there seemed no obvious reason why the mobile was moving. "Stop!" commanded my host. The mobile stopped. "Reverse," he called out. The mobile began to spin in the opposite direction. "I don't have to point," he told me. "That was only to show you I was doing something. I can move it just by thinking at it. Pick a direction, clockwise or anticlockwise."

For the next ten minutes or so, I told my host exactly how I wanted the mobile to move and when I wanted it to stop. The thing on the ceiling followed orders with the precision of a military recruit. "This is extraordinary," I said eventually. "Have you tried anything else?"

He shook his head. "I haven't dared. This sort of thing makes my wife nervous and she's forbidden me to do it. I shouldn't even be showing you."

Since this curious experience, I've suspected there may be many more people than we might imagine who can move things with their minds, people who, by reason of nervous wives or whatever, prefer to keep the ability a secret, or people who have never even thought of trying.

If you think you might be one of them, here's a piece of apparatus you can make that will let you test the ability for yourself. What you'll need is a cork, a needle and a piece of lightweight silver paper.

Cigarette smoking is a lot less acceptable than it used to be, but if you can still find somebody with the habit, you'll find exactly the right weight of silver paper inside the packet. All you need is the bit that smokers throw away when they open a fresh pack – it's about the right size for what you have to do. (You could use a piece of kitchen foil – it has to be light though.)

Carefully strip off the backing tissue so you're left with undamaged silver paper. Fold and cut it so it forms a square. Now crease the square by folding along its diagonals and again top to bottom, then side to side. When you open it flat again, it should look like this:

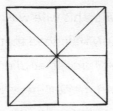

Now a little light origami. Using the diagram below as a guide, fold the creased square so it forms a little tent.

You can leave your little tent aside now for the moment. Take your needle and poke it in the cork (left, below) then carefully balance the tent on top as shown.

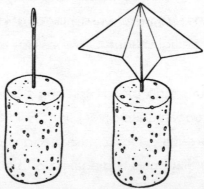

What you've made is a miniature mobile, a lot less decorative, but similar in function, to the one my host moved when his wife wasn't watching. The silver tent is so finely balanced that it will spin freely when the slightest force is applied to it including, hopefully, your own mental energy.

To carry out your first experiment, set the device up on a table in front of you. Leave it for a moment to make sure there are no draughts that might start it spinning, then sit down, place your hands to either side of it and concentrate. Don't strain. PK often shows itself more quickly if you're in a relaxed state. If you're lucky – and have the power – the tent will first tremble slightly, then begin to spin.

Once you've achieved a straightforward spin, see if you can will the tent to stop. Now try to spin it in the opposite direction. With practice, you may be able to control it as effectively as my host controlled his bedroom mobile.

Chapter 18

Full circle

So now we've come full circle – from Russia and Wolf Messing on a round-the-world tour of weirdness back to Russia again and Ninel Kulagina. But does this trip exhaust the strange powers of the human mind? Not at all, it hardly scratches the surface.

We might, for example, have taken time to examine precognition, the incredible ability to see into the future. Dr Rhine tested for it the same way he tested for telepathy, by using Zener cards. He discovered there were a few rare individuals who could consistently guess not the card that was currently being transmitted to them, but the one that was about to be turned up from the deck. As with telepathy, the odds against chance as an explanation for these guesses were, in some cases, astronomical.

Rhine's subjects were only able to see a second or two into the future (although in theory a second or two is just as impossible as a year or two), but there are clearly recorded instances in history of people who could see ahead for decades. The 16th century French prophet Nostradamus, for example, accurately predicted the exact date of the French Revolution (1793) even though it occurred more than two centuries after he was dead. Nor was he the only one. A contemporary astrologer got it spot on as well.

Or we might have looked at the strange workings behind curses. Australian Aborigines have repeatedly demonstrated the reality behind their tradition of the Clever Man (witch-doctor) and his pointing bone. According to the stories, a tribesperson who *really* gets on the wrong side of a Clever Man might find himself pointed at by a specially sharpened piece of bone. The action is believed to be a death sentence and the victim will typically sicken mysteriously and die.

Western doctors, helplessly watching the curse in action, generally insist it's all a question of suggestion – the aborigine *believes* the Clever Man has the power to kill him and it's this very belief that causes him to die. But the distinguished novelist John Cowper Powys discovered to his horror that people he hated had a habit of dying suddenly. Thereafter he had to live his life in a state of extreme goodwill towards everyone to avoid leaving a string of corpses in his wake. The writer Colin Wilson also confessed to similar occurrences in his own life, although not nearly so extreme. The point about this is that suggestion clearly doesn't come into it, since many of Powys's 'victims' were unaware of his feelings.

And then there's the problem of eyeless sight, or 'dermo-optic vision' as the investigating scientists like to call it. Some people, including at least one who has been blind from birth and lacked an optic nerve, have trained themselves to see with the tips of their fingers or other parts of their bodies.

As any scientist will tell you, it's absolutely,

totally, wholly impossible for skin cells to react to light with sufficient sensitivity to read a book, yet that's exactly what's been happening in certain cases – a rare example of yet another strange power.

The list of weirdnesses marches on. You may think of yourself as a single person – and you may even be right. But there are some poor souls whose bodies are occupied by two, five, ten and in some cases even scores of different people. Psychiatrists refer to the condition as 'multiple personality disorder' and generally believe it represents a single personality that shattered into pieces due to shock or abuse.

The trouble with this theory is that the 'pieces' don't act like pieces. They pop in and out like visitors to an open house, each complete in himself with memories, knowledge and abilities the others don't share. In some cases of multiple personality disorder, a tough guy will emerge to protect others sharing the body when a threat arises.

The mind is unknown territory and even some familiar powers have very spooky aspects. One example is dowsing, the ability to find underground water using no more than a forked stick. For dowsers – and many more people have the ability than you'd think – the forked stick, held in a state of tension, will dip when they walk over an underground stream.

Scientists have long since explained this (to their own satisfaction) by pointing out that there are many geological signs of underground water and while the dowser may not be *consciously* aware of them, his unconscious mind notes the signs and causes the stick to dip. It makes great sense, except that some people can dowse using only maps (which have no geological signs whatsoever) while others don't bother with water, but dowse for oil, gold, lost objects and even unknown prehistoric sites.

Perhaps the strangest thing of all is something called synchronicity, a term that translates as 'meaningful coincidence.' You've probably experienced it yourself at some time in your life. Perhaps you're walking down the street when you encounter a man with a sandwich-board advertising a play called *'Watch Out For Fred'*. Moments later, you turn a corner and almost bump into your old friend Fred whom you haven't seen in years...

Coincidences like that – and a great deal stranger – really happen. Or perhaps, are really *caused*. Carl Jung, the psychologist who made a study of synchronicity (and coined the term) believed it to be yet another weird example of the strange powers of the human mind.

You can do it

Somebody remarked on radio the other morning that the days of the great amateur scientific breakthroughs were now gone. To make advances in physics you needed equipment costing millions of pounds and nobody got anywhere in any of the sciences without a hefty research grant.

I'm not sure that's really true — the greatest advances in physics during the past 100 years were made by Albert Einstein using equipment (a pencil and paper) that cost him tuppence — but even if it is, it doesn't hold good for psychical research.

If there's been anything in this book that's intrigued you about the strange powers of the human mind, you're remarkably well-placed to do some ground-breaking research yourself.

For a start, you have a fully-equipped laboratory right there inside your head. You can study your own abilities, observe your own mental processes, test your own powers with no more investment than a little time and effort.

Start with something simple. Try staring at the back of somebody's neck and see how long it takes them to turn round. Or try guessing who's calling when the phone rings. Or note how often your dog's waiting for you at the door when you come home unexpectedly.

As your results build up and your interest develops, you can go on to more complicated things, maybe even make yourself a deck of Zener cards or programme your computer (BASIC is good) to test for precognition or clairvoyance.

Research of this sort isn't very fashionable these days, but it's a lot more beneficial to the human race than building bigger bombs.

And you can do it. Starting now. What's more, you can be the one to make the next huge breakthrough.

Further reading

Dreaming to Some Purpose, Colin Wilson, Century Books, London, 2004.

Frankenstein's Castle, Colin Wilson, Ashgrove Press, Sevenoaks, 1980.

Harper's Encyclopedia of Mystical and Paranormal Experience, Rosemary Ellen Guiley, Harper San Francisco, 1991.

Mindreach, J. H. Brennan, Aquarian Press, Wellingborough, 1985.

Open to Suggestion, Robert Temple, Aquarian Press, 1989.

Psychic Discoveries Behind the Iron Curtain, Sheila Ostrander and Lynn Schroeder, Bantam Books, New York, 1971.

Psychical Research Today, D. J. West, Pelican Books, London, 1962.

Ritual Magic in England, (1887 to the Present Day), Francis King, Neville Spearman, London, 1970.

Science and the Paranormal, Arthur J. Ellison, Floris Books, Edinburgh, 2002.

Supernature II, Lyall Watson, Sceptre Books, London, 1986.

The Encyclopedia of Parapsychology and Psychical Research, Arthur S and Joyce Berger, Paragon House, New York, 1991.

The Golden Dawn, Israel Regardie, Llewellyn Publications, St Paul, MS, 1993.

The Projection of the Astral Body, Sylvan Muldoon and Hereward Carrington, Rider & Co, London, 1989

Index

Aborigine 185-186

Aitken, Professor A.C 43-
44, 48

animal magnetism 23-24,
75

Associative Remote
Viewing (ARV) 133-134

astrology 20

Barrett, William 75-77

Batcheldor, Kenneth 160-
171

Birchall, James 79

Blitzkrieg 10

Burgess, Jacquie 134

Carrington, Hereward, 141,
143, 144, 146

Cayce, Edgar 53-59

Charcot, Jean-Martin 34

Chrysanthius 148

clairvoyance 51, 132, 191

Cold War 96

Creery, A.M. 74-75, 77

Crowley, Aleister 112-114,
116

David-Neel, Alexandra 117-
123

dermo-optic vision 186

Donkin, Dr Horatio 81

dowsing 187-188

Einstein, Albert 190

Ellison, Arthur J. 134, 144

Extra Sensory Perception
(ESP) 86

eyeless sight 186

FBI 89-91

Freemasons 113

French Revolution 185

Freud, Dr Sigmund 50

Golden Dawn, Hermetic
Students of 113-116, 121,
124, 126, 127, 128, 140

Gurdieff, G. I. 111

Guthrie, Malcolm 79, 83

Hailey, Alex 44

Heroditus 127

hieroglyphs 113

Hitler, Adolf 9, 15

Home, Daniel Dunglas 154-156

hypnosis 19, 20, 28, 29-42, 50, 51-55, 57-59, 60, 64-65, 71, 76, 96, 98, 111, 112

Iamblichus 148

Jacolliot, Louis 149
Jung, Karl 189

kabbalah 113
KGB 16
Kremlin 17
Kulagina, Ninel 174-179, 184
kylkhor 123-125

Layne, Al 55-58
levitation 147-156, 162-163, 165-166
leeches 21-22
Luria, A. R. 45, 48

magnet 21-24, 174-175
Mahadevan, Rajan 44
mekhenesis 30
Mesmer, Franz Anton, 20-28, 29, 91-92, 132

Messing, Wolf 9-19, 42, 71, 72, 86-87, 92, 98, 184
mind-training 114
Moll, Albert 82-83
Muldoon, Sylvan 141-144
multiple personality disorder 187
muscle-reading 13, 74

Nostradamus 185

oracle 127-129, 131
Osis, Karlis 145
Out-of-Body Experience (OOB) 136, 140-141, 144-146, 147

Penfield, Dr Wilder 48-49
perpetual pill 21-22
prerecognition 184, 191
psychoanalysis 50
psychokinesis (PK) 174, 179, 183
pointing bone 185
post-hypnotic amnesia 41
post-hypnotic suggestion 41
post-hypnotic trigger 36
Powys, John Cowper 186
Puthoff, Hal 132

Puységur, Marquis de 29,
91

Raikov, Dr Vladimir L. 60,
62-71
Rasputin 109-111
remote viewing 128-129,
131, 133-136, 144
Rhine, Joseph Banks 83-84,
86, 172-174, 184-185
Russian Revolution 109

seance 155, 165
Second World War 16
Sheldrake, Rupert 78
Society for Psychical
Research 77, 81, 92, 134
Spiritualism 57, 155
Stalin, Josef 15-19, 71, 87,
92, 99
Swedenborg, Emanuel 129-
132
synchronicity 188-189
synesthesia 48

Targ, Russel 132
Tart, Charles 144-145
telepathic drawings 80
telepathy 12, 77-78, 81, 83,
86, 92, 93, 96,184

Temple, Robert 105
thought-form 120, 123, 126
thought-transference 74
Tibet 117-126, 127, 148
trance 30, 32-39, 41, 55-58,
63-67, 70-71, 75-76, 95-99,
106, 130, 156
tulpa 120-123

visualisation 115, 122, 124-
125, 140, 148
Wilson, Colin 186

Yeats, W. B. 113
yidam 123-125

Zener pack/deck/cards 85-
86, 184, 191,
Zodiac, Signs of the 114